BookShots / Little, Brown and Company
Hachette Book Group
1290 Avenue of the Americas, New York, NY 10104
bookshots.com

First Edition: January 2017

BookShots is an imprint of Little, Brown and Company, a division of Hachette Book Group, Inc. The Little, Brown name and logo are trademarks of Hachette Book Group, Inc. The BookShots name and logo are trademarks of JBP Business, LLC.

The publisher is not responsible for websites (or their content) that are not owned by the publisher.

The Hachette Speakers Bureau provides a wide range of authors for speaking events. To find out more, go to hachettespeakersbureau.com or call (866) 376-6591.

ISBN 978-0-316-27661-0
LCCN 2016943247

10 9 8 7 6 5 4 3 2

LSC-H

Printed in the United States of America

AVAILABLE NOW!

LEARNING TO RIDE

City girl Madeline Harper never wanted to love a cowboy. But rodeo king Tanner Callen might change her mind…and win her heart.

THE McCULLAGH INN IN MAINE

Chelsea O'Kane escapes to Maine to build a new life—until she runs into Jeremy Holland, an old flame.…

SACKING THE QUARTERBACK

Attorney Melissa St. James wins every case. Now, when she's up against football superstar Grayson Knight, her heart is on the line, too.

THE MATING SEASON

Documentary ornithologist Sophie Castle is convinced that her heart belongs only to the birds—until she meets her gorgeous cameraman, Rigg Greensman.

THE RETURN

Ashley Montoya was in love with Mack McLeroy in high school—until he broke her heart. But when an accident brings him back home to Sunnybell to recover, Ashley can't help but fall into his embrace....

BODYGUARD
Special Agent Abbie Whitmore has only one task: protect Congressman Jonathan Lassiter from a violent cartel's threats. Yet she's never had to do it while falling in love....

DAZZLING: THE DIAMOND TRILOGY, BOOK I
To support her artistic career, Siobhan Dempsey works at the elite Stone Room in New York City...never expecting to be swept away by Derick Miller.

RADIANT: THE DIAMOND TRILOGY, BOOK II
After an explosive breakup with her billionaire boyfriend, Siobhan moves to Detroit to pursue her art. But Derick isn't ready to give her up.

EXQUISITE: THE DIAMOND TRILOGY, BOOK III
Siobhan's artistic career is finally successful, and she's ready to start a life with her billionaire boyfriend Derick. But their relationship has been a rollercoaster ride, and Derick may not want her after all....

HOT WINTER NIGHTS
Allie Fairchild moved to Montana to start fresh as the head of the trauma center. And even though the days are cold, the nights are steamy...especially when she meets search-and-rescue leader D Belmont.

A WEDDING IN MAINE
Chelsea O'Kane is ready to marry Jeremy Holland in the in they've built together—until the secrets of her past refuse to st buried. And they could ruin everything.

BOOKSHOTS

CROSS KILL
Along Came a Spider killer Gary Soneji died years ago. But Ale Cross swears he sees Soneji gun down his partner. Is his greates enemy back from the grave?

ZOO 2
Humans are evolving into a savage new species that could save civilization—or end it. James Patterson's *Zoo* was just the beginning.

THE TRIAL
An accused killer will do anything to disrupt his own trial, including a courtroom shocker that Lindsay Boxer and the Women's Murder Club will never see coming.

FOREWORD

Hello there, BookShots Flames reader. You're a special breed of reader, and I'm glad you've picked up this book. Look, I know your life is busy. Maybe you're in between two longer works of fiction, or maybe you can only find the time to read during your commute or right before you go to bed. Or maybe you don't care about the length of a story and are just looking for a good read. But whatever your reason for making this purchase, I hope you enjoy it.

Because if you're the type of reader I think you are, I have a feeling you like books with lots of action. I bet you don't like to be bored. I'm guessing you like stories that have surprises around every corner, and twists tucked into their plots. And I know that I can give you that in this book, and in any of the books we're publishing with BookShots.

But you're a BookShots Flames reader. You're looking for even more than that. Underneath those shocking plots that keep you on your toes, you like a book with a nice love story. You want to discover soul mates finding each other and enjoy the fireworks show when characters fall in love. You crave romance, and I can't say I blame you, because I, too, know that love makes the world go 'round.

And now here you are, at the final chapter in Siobhan and Derick's journey. You know that things haven't been easy for them. It's been hard for Siobhan to trust Derick, and then the distance made things even more difficult for their relationship. There's a good chance that, since Derick bought Siobhan that gallery, these two are never going to get back together. But you also know the power of love, and are just a little bit curious about whether these two can make it. So go on, turn the page. Let's give them a final shot.

James Patterson

Exquisite

Chapter 1

SIOBHAN BLEW OUT a frustrated breath and threw her phone into her bag.

The girls eyed one another cautiously, as if the wrong question might break her completely. A few moments of silence passed before finally one of them spoke.

"What did he say?" Blaine asked quietly.

Siobhan leaned her head back against the cushion of Cory's couch and stared at the ceiling. "Nothing. What *can* he say? I barely even gave him a chance to speak." She brought her head down to look at her friends and saw worry written on their faces. "The only reason I answered was so he'd stop calling."

"Do you think he knows why you're not going to the airport?" Marnel asked. "You didn't even mention the gallery."

"He's an idiot, but he can't be *that* dumb. He has to know that I found out about the gallery. What other reason would there be for me to act like this?" She propped her elbows on her knees and settled her chin on her hands pensively.

"And you know what?" Siobhan could hear her voice getting louder, angrier. "I really don't care what he knows or doesn't know. I'm done giving a shit about how he feels because he clearly doesn't give a shit about how *I* feel. If he did, he wouldn't have bought a goddamn art gallery for me without even speaking to me about it first." Siobhan stood and headed toward Cory's kitchen. "You got anything to drink?"

"There's iced tea in the fridge."

Siobhan turned back toward the girls. Her expression must have been enough to tell them that iced tea wasn't going to be strong enough.

"And vodka in the freezer," Cory added.

Siobhan pulled the bottle out and held it up. "Anyone else want any?"

The girls shook their heads. "We have to work in a few hours," Marnel said.

"Guess it'll be a party of one then," Siobhan said, closing the freezer door and heading back to the couch with just the bottle. She took the cap off and plopped down onto the couch. She stared ahead for a minute before bringing the bottle to her lips and taking a long pull.

"I can't believe I thought he'd change," she said, shaking her head. "Or that he *did* change. He had to have known how I'd react, and he still bought that gallery. And more than that, he kept it a fucking secret. Was he gonna sell my work like it didn't even mean anything to him? I mean, Jesus Christ, it's not like he needs the money. None of it makes any sense."

Siobhan could hear herself rambling, but she didn't care. She needed to purge her thoughts.

Marnel scooted over on the couch to wrap her in a hug. "I'm sorry," she said without elaborating, but Siobhan knew what she meant. She was sorry it didn't work out with Derick. Sorry that he kept making the same mistakes over and over again. Sorry that Derick hurt her.

Siobhan was sorry, too.

"I literally told him *this morning* that I'd consider moving back to New York if things between us were good for the next six months. Then, just like that, he had to go and mess everything up again."

"Well, to be fair, he'd already messed it up," Blaine said. "But you didn't know."

Siobhan glared at her.

"Sorry," Blaine said, looking contrite. She held out her hand for Siobhan to pass her the bottle. "I can't watch you day-drink alone. It's sad." Blaine put the bottle to her lips for a swig and then handed it back to her friend.

Siobhan shrugged. "If the shoe fits."

Cory got up and returned with four glasses, taking the bottle from Siobhan and pouring a double shot for each of them. "Screw it. We didn't have lunch yet. Might as well make it a liquid one."

Marnel picked up her glass. "Yeah. We'll be sober by the time we have to go to work."

"Or not." Blaine gave Siobhan a comforting smile, silently letting her know they were there for her when she needed them the most. "What's Saul gonna do? Fire *all* of us before our shift even starts?"

"He'll probably wait until after we close," Cory said, making Siobhan laugh for the first time since she'd found out about the gallery. "I knew there was a smile in you somewhere."

"So what are you gonna do now?" Marnel asked.

"I'm gonna drink the rest of this," Siobhan said, feeling a bit stronger than she had earlier. "Then tomorrow I'm gonna fly back to Detroit and get on with my life as if none of this ever happened."

"Sounds like a solid plan." Blaine gave her a nod of approval. "To Detroit," she said, raising her glass and prompting the others to do the same.

"To Detroit," Cory and Siobhan both repeated as they all clinked glasses.

"Uh-uh." Marnel shook her head. "To Siobhan."

"To Siobhan," Blaine and Cory said.

And for the second time since they'd gotten to Cory's, Siobhan smiled.

Chapter 2

PULLING HER EARBUDS out, Siobhan looked around the terminal. She could have sworn she'd heard her name over the loudspeaker. She grabbed her purse and carry-on bag and walked up to the small desk near the gate. "Excuse me. Did I get paged?"

The woman looked up from the computer and tucked her silky black hair behind her ear. "Siobhan Dempsey?"

Siobhan nodded. *Don't even tell me this flight's overbooked and they're gonna ask me to give up my seat.*

The woman reached under the counter and handed Siobhan a manila envelope. "This is for you."

Siobhan's eyebrows furrowed in confusion. "What is it?"

The woman shook her head and shrugged. "No idea," she replied.

"Okay, thanks," Siobhan said, turning around to return to her seat. She plopped down again and put her bags on the empty chair next to her.

She pulled up the metal prongs and unsealed the envelope to remove the few pieces of white paper that were inside. "You've got to be kidding me," she whispered, her voice coming out in an annoyed huff.

She studied the paper closely, making sure it was what she thought. Then she put the papers back into the envelope and shoved it into her carry-on.

Chapter 3

DERICK PULLED HIS phone out of his pocket and looked at it. "Excuse me," he said, standing up from the conference table. "I need to take this." He pushed the thick glass door open and stepped out into the hallway. There was no way he would let Siobhan's call go to voice mail, even though he was certain that their conversation wouldn't be pleasant. He might as well get it over with.

He answered the call and put the phone to his ear. "Hello," he said.

"What the hell is this?" was the response.

"What's what?"

"The deed to the gallery."

Derick kept his voice even. "It sounds like you already know what it is. Did you need something else?" He knew his response was terse, but he didn't care. She hadn't even given him the chance to explain, and here she was calling, clearly angry.

Siobhan was silent for a moment, and then he heard her blow out an agitated breath. "Yeah. I need you to tell me what you expect me to do with it. You just send me the deed to a gallery you bought, and—" She paused. "I'm not even going to ask how you knew what flight I'd be on."

Despite the context, Derick couldn't help but smile.

"I'm flying back to Detroit, Derick. What the hell am I supposed to do with an art gallery in New York?"

Derick put a hand in his pocket. "I'm not sure," he said simply. "Sell it, run it, have someone run it *for* you."

"I'm glad you gave this a lot of thought," she spat.

Derick drew in a calming breath. Though he tried to suppress it, he could feel the sadness in his throat. "Giving you the deed was a loose end I needed to tie up. The gallery's yours, Siobhan. It was always supposed to be yours. You can do whatever you'd like with it."

For a moment, there was silence on the other end of the line until Siobhan sighed heavily. "I'm just so tired of fighting."

"You said it yourself. It's done. There's nothing to fight about anymore." He paused to let his words carry the weight he hoped they had. "I have to get back to a meeting," he said. "I have people waiting for me."

"Okay," she said. Her voice was small, but somehow, it wasn't weak.

"I'll talk to you later." Rubbing his hairline, he shook his head. "Actually, I guess I won't. In any case, if you have questions about the property, feel free to call the number I provided on the deed. That's my lawyer's line. She can help you with anything you need."

"Okay," she said again.

"Enjoy the gallery, Siobhan."

Chapter 4

YOU LIKE THAT one?" Jacob nodded toward the oak table Siobhan had been running her hand across.

She turned toward him. "I like *all* of it. I can't believe anyone can make pieces like this." She knew he was talented, but seeing all of his furniture in one place was more impressive than she'd anticipated. "It's one thing to paint or sculpt, but it's another to be able to create art that actually has a function."

Wendell pointed toward a bedframe on the other side of the boutique. "You ever bang on that bed?" he asked.

Jacob lifted an eyebrow, letting Wendell know how ridiculous his question was. "It doesn't even have a mattress on it."

Wendell shrugged. "Still. If it were mine, I'd have to screw someone on it at least once before I sold it." He popped another piece of cheese into his mouth. "You gotta christen that shit."

Lilah's voice floated their way as she approached them. "Did you leave any food for the guests?" she asked.

Wendell looked confused. "Uh, I *am* a guest."

"I meant the customers, you doofus," Lilah said. "You're just a friend. The opening isn't really for *us*."

Siobhan ignored her friends' playful bickering and admired the sleek lines and the asymmetry of the chairbacks. "I really can't get over how incredible your work is."

"Thanks. I'm glad all of you could make it tonight." Jacob smiled proudly before excusing himself to go greet a customer who'd come in.

Siobhan smiled back, but it felt empty. The thought of Jacob's boutique opening to the public only reminded her of the gallery she owned back in New York.

It felt shitty to be celebrating someone's happiness when she didn't feel happy herself. But that line of logic only made her feel like a shitty friend. And thinking she was a shitty friend made her feel even shittier. It was a vicious cycle.

"You've been weird since you got back." Lilah bumped her hip against Siobhan's.

"She was always weird," Wendell said.

Lilah rolled her eyes. "I'm serious. You all right?" she asked Siobhan.

Siobhan's first instinct was to lie. She could say she was fine—that she was just tired or overwhelmed or felt like she was getting the beginning of a cold. But if Lilah could tell Siobhan was acting odd, it must have been really obvious. Lilah was the quintessential artistic space cadet. "Not really," Siobhan replied.

Lilah grabbed a glass of wine from the table nearby and handed it to Siobhan. "Spill it, Brooklyn."

"I'm assuming you don't mean the wine."

Lilah stared at her.

Siobhan rolled her eyes and released a long breath before she spoke. "Derick and I broke up. It's a long story."

Lilah shrugged. "I got time."

Wendell suddenly looked uncomfortable, like he'd just walked in on his parents having sex. Clearly plotting his escape, his eyes darted to different spots in the boutique. Listening to Siobhan's girl problems was probably the last thing he wanted to do. "Uh... I have something... I have to—"

"It's fine, Wendell. You can go," Lilah said, shaking her head. Once he was gone, Lilah looked at Siobhan expectantly. "What happened?"

Starting at the beginning, Siobhan told Lilah all of it: how Derick's wealth had always intimidated her, how he'd bought the first paintings she'd ever sold. She hadn't shared any of that with anyone she'd met in Detroit, choosing instead to leave New York and everything associated with it behind her.

Detroit had been her escape from the bad memories. But now Derick had tainted that city, too. "He bought the building, Lilah."

Lilah looked confused.

"The one with the mural. He renovated it into office space and some gigantic loft apartment that cost him God only knows how much."

"How did he even know about it? Did he even try to explain any of it before you broke up with him?"

Siobhan drew in a deep breath. "That's not why I broke up with him."

Lilah's eyes widened. "Jesus, what else is there? What'd he buy, the whole city for you?"

Siobhan shook her head. "A gallery in New York."

"Seriously?"

"Seriously."

Lilah bit her bottom lip pensively. "Soooo…I gotta be honest, Brooklyn. That's pretty awesome."

"It doesn't feel awesome. I found out when I walked by it on my way to lunch with some friends. It's hard not to notice your own paintings hanging in a store window."

"Yeah, but…" Lilah looked cautious, uncertain of the right thing to say. "It's kind of a sweet gesture, don't you think? Maybe he was waiting to surprise you."

Siobhan glared at her. "I can't believe you're taking his side on this."

"I'm not 'taking his side.' I just…I don't know. There are worse things for a boyfriend to do than buy extravagant gifts for his girl-friend."

"It's not the cost that bothers me. Derick should know by now that I want to succeed on my own. I thought he learned from his mistake when I moved out here. But he doesn't get it, and he never will." Siobhan could hear the irritation in her voice, but she didn't try to hide it. "I don't want his help," she said, releasing an exasperated breath. "I don't *need* it."

"Sorry," Jacob interjected. "I wasn't trying to listen to your conversation, but I couldn't help but overhear. Derick bought you a gallery?" he asked. He looked almost…excited.

"Yeah. Please don't tell me that you're going to defend him, too."

Jacob pushed up his shirtsleeves and put a hand in his pocket. "No, I'm not going to defend him. This isn't really about Derick. It's about you."

"Well, yeah, I know it's about me." Siobhan was confused.

"Look, it took me almost ten years of trying to open this boutique before it finally happened. And it didn't just *happen*. I had to apprentice for a grumpy hard-ass for three years. I basically did everything for him except wipe his ass."

"Why didn't you quit? You're talented. You shouldn't have had to put up with that."

Jacob shrugged. "I learned pretty quickly that talent wasn't enough. The guy had connections that I didn't have. And even though he was a complete dick most of the time, he knew what he was doing. I learned a lot from him. When it came down to it, he believed in me. He helped me get the boutique up and running."

"I never even knew you apprenticed," Siobhan said.

"I probably never mentioned it because by the time you moved here, I was already in the process of opening the store. That's huge that you have a gallery in New York. That's a pretty great accomplishment for an artist."

Siobhan sighed heavily. "Yeah, but *I* didn't open it. Someone opened it *for* me."

"Look," Jacob continued. "I get where you're coming from with the whole wanting to do it on your own stuff. There's definitely a certain amount of pride that comes with making it by yourself, especially in the art field because so many people don't view it as a career."

"Exactly," Siobhan agreed.

"But…no one gets anywhere without help from *someone*," Jacob added. "Family members, friends, teachers, whoever. No one succeeds completely on their own." Jacob laughed softly and ran a hand along the carefully groomed scruff on his face. "I mean, most people don't get a New York City gallery given to them, but that doesn't mean you shouldn't take it."

He paused to pop a grape into his mouth. "You have to put your ego aside and do what's best for *you* and your career. If you want to make a living off your art, you need to take every opportunity that's given to you."

Lilah finished chewing the bread she had in her mouth before she spoke. "That's exactly what I was trying to tell her."

Siobhan glared at her humorlessly. "You didn't say *any* of that."

"Whatever," Lilah replied. "Semantics."

Jacob shrugged. "Even if you decide to run the gallery, there's no guarantee it'll succeed. If you don't have enough talent to sustain a painting career, you'll fail anyway."

"Well, that's comforting," Siobhan said.

He chuckled quietly before his expression grew more serious. "Take the gallery."

Chapter 5

UNCLE DERICK," LOGAN yelled as he ran to the front door at lightning speed. "Dad said you flew a helicopter here. Can I sit in it?"

Derick shook his head and rolled his eyes at his brother, who was standing in the foyer laughing quietly.

"I don't have a helicopter, Logan. Your dad's being silly."

"Oh," Logan replied, looking slightly disappointed. "You should get one then."

Derick smiled at his nephew and gave the five-year-old a few playful punches to his stomach. "I'll think about it, okay?"

"'Kay," Logan replied. "You should get a green one." Then he took off toward the kitchen as quickly as he'd come in.

Derick looked at Cole and chuckled. "You'd lie to your own kid to mess with me? You're an asshole, you know that?"

Cole smiled. "I do."

"Hi, Derick." Melissa glided gracefully toward him. He wrapped his arms around his sister-in-law and gave her a kiss. Her red hair had gotten considerably longer since he'd seen her last.

"You look great. I can't believe you're gonna have a baby in a few months. You're not even that big," he said, pulling back to look at her.

Cole winced at his brother's words, as if he knew what was coming.

"Not *that* big?" Melissa asked, smacking his chest. "What does that mean?"

Shit. "I just meant that…I thought you'd be like, really huge. But you're not. You're…" Unsure of how to finish his sentence, he stared awkwardly at her.

Melissa shook her head at him. "I'll be in the kitchen. Dinner will probably be ready in a half hour or so. Try not to get into too much trouble before then."

"We're not making any promises," Cole said as she walked off. Then he turned back toward Derick. "You're such an idiot."

Derick laughed as he took off his jacket and tossed it on the railing. "So I've been told."

Cole opened the basement door. "Come downstairs. I gotta show you what I did to it. It's a man cave on steroids," he said as he trotted down the steps.

Derick followed him downstairs. "This is pretty sweet," he said, admiring the masculine space. He ran a hand along the granite bar. "You think this is gonna get any use? You have a five-year-old and you'll have a newborn soon."

Cole turned to stare at him like Derick was a moron. "That's *exactly* why it'll be used. I need an escape from whatever…that is up there," Cole said, pointing toward the ceiling. "It sounds like the running of the bulls." His face grew serious. "That's *one* kid, Derick. I'm gonna have two soon." He ran a panicked hand through his dark hair. "What the hell was I thinking?"

"It'll be fine," Derick assured him.

"Says the man with no wife or children." Cole grabbed two beers out of the small fridge and handed one to his brother.

Derick laughed. "We have time for a game, right?" he asked, pointing at the pool table.

Cole grabbed Derick's arm. "I have time for nothing. I can't even take a shit without Logan banging on the door because he wants to show me some video about the respiratory system or something." He grabbed a cue and lined up to break. "Seriously. What kid looks at medical videos for fun? I'm tellin' you," he said, pointing his stick at Derick. "Something's not right with him. He's like…"

"Smart?" Derick said.

"I was thinking more like nerdy. Wait until he gets to first grade. That's when kids really start noticing when their classmates are weird. It's only a matter of time before they rub his face in the dirt or dangle him out the window of the bus."

Derick rolled his eyes. "He's going to elementary school, not rushing a frat. They're not gonna torture him. You're being dramatic."

"No way," Cole said. "Kids are cruel. And soon I'm gonna have a daughter. I know nothing about girls, Derick. Nothing!"

"Well, you definitely know more than me because you managed to get one to marry you." Derick sank the six ball in the corner pocket and moved to the side of the table to line up his next shot.

"I know," Cole said. "And she's hot. I'm still not sure why she said yes."

"Clearly she's a glutton for punishment," Derick joked.

"I guess Siobhan is, too," Cole shot back with a smile. But it quickly disappeared when he seemed to notice Derick's jovial expression fade. "Jesus. What'd you do now?"

Derick chalked up his stick, not wanting to make eye contact with Cole. "Does it matter?"

"Well, I have to know what you did if I'm gonna help you fix it."

From the moment when the call with Siobhan had ended, Derick knew it was over for good. But this time it wasn't because Siobhan wouldn't take him back. This time *he* was done. Done chasing her, done apologizing to her, done trying to convince her that he meant well. "It's over, Cole. I don't want to fix it."

ouch

o the

def-

ould

hing.

n was

know

u?"

ong,"

much

I'm in

nd off

asked

ack to

to run

Chapter 6

ED THE last box onto the creaky wooden

hat much stuff," Dom commented as he

that she'd moved into.

before I left Detroit. I knew there wouldn't

he said. "This place is cute, though. And it's

in the city. I lived in Brooklyn last time."

asked. "I didn't know you'd lived in New

told me was that she had a friend who was

led a place. I haven't had a roommate in a

initely happy to be splitting the rent again."

to follow him. "Let me show you around."

anyone who wanted to rent it?" Siobhan

hind him.

ted. I didn't want to rent it to some random

ived here before you was strange as shit. I

in the six months he lived here. He'd sleep

d stuff."

Siobhan laughed. "I definitely won't be sleeping on the ‹ nude," she assured him.

Dom pointed to the small fridge and oven. "Not much ‹ kitchen, but everything works."

She nodded.

"And for the record," Dom said, "the sleeping naked thir initely wouldn't be as creepy to me if *you* did it."

Siobhan knew a comment like that from a stranger s make her uncomfortable, but for some reason it had her lau

Dom took her to the basement where the laundry roo and then gave her a key to the apartment. "So how do you Blaine?" he asked as he took a seat on the small sofa.

"We worked at the Stone Room together. What about y

"We went to high school together," Dom said.

"Oh, wow. I didn't realize you've known each other that Siobhan said.

"Yeah, like fifteen years, I guess it's been. I don't see her anymore, but we keep in touch through Facebook and stuff finance, so I'm basically married to work during the week ; on the weekends. Our schedules don't really match up."

"Gotcha," Siobhan said. "Is it weird that neither of u anything about the other before we agreed to live together

"Probably." Dom laughed. "So what made you move ‹ New York?"

"I'm a painter," she said confidently. "And I moved back a gallery."

Chapter 7

SIOBHAN UNWOUND THE scarf from around her neck as she entered the Stone Room. A flood of memories tried to surface, causing a prickling behind her eyes that she thankfully hadn't felt since moving back to New York. At least not often. The place triggered memories of all the Dericks Siobhan had encountered: the chivalrous one, the stubborn one, the sweet one, the possessive one. The one she still loved a little, but hated a little bit, too.

Basically, being back in the club made her uneasy, and Siobhan wanted to collect the girls and get the hell out of there.

The plan was to go to an after-hours bar Blaine had worked some kind of bartender magic to get them invited to. It was supposedly as exclusive as the Stone Room, while also being more inclusive. Anyone could go as long as you were on the list that Blaine had said was guarded by enormous bouncers and a velvet rope. Siobhan was pretty damn excited.

"You can't be in here unless you're working. And I'm pretty sure I fired you months ago."

Oh, for Christ's sake. Siobhan plastered a smile on her face and turned slowly. "Hi, Saul. Long time no see. And you didn't fire me. I finally came to my senses and quit this dive," she said. But then she analyzed the look on Saul's face and realized it was warm and kind.

He stepped closer and leaned in to peck Siobhan on the cheek. He seemed genuinely pleased to see her and Siobhan wondered if the man had undergone a lobotomy since she'd seen him last. "Howya doin', kid? I heard you were back in town."

"Yup, I'm back." The response was lame, but Siobhan wasn't really sure what else to say.

"Well, it's good to see you." His smile suddenly dropped. "You're not here looking for a job, are you? Because I finally managed to rebuild our crystal stemware collection."

Siobhan bit back a smile. "You're really funny tonight. Spending some quality time in the liquor closet again?"

Saul let out a hearty laugh.

"I'm just waiting for the girls," Siobhan explained.

Saul looked around the club. "They should be about done. I'll let them know you're here."

"Thanks, Saul."

He started to walk away, but turned back toward her after he'd taken a few steps. "And I was just teasing you. It really is great to see you here."

He left before she could reply, which was a good thing because his words had choked her up a bit. She really was becoming a basket case.

Siobhan waited at the front for a little while longer before she heard her friends in all their rowdy glory making their way toward her.

"I don't get why you care *how* I got us in. Just be thankful I was able to," Siobhan heard Blaine saying.

"No, there's something fishy going on. And if I have to get you drunk to find out what it is, so be it," Marnel replied.

"You're going to take advantage of a drunk girl? Where's your sense of sisterhood?" Blaine argued.

"Don't have any."

Blaine and Cory burst into laughter as they walked up to Siobhan and hugged her.

"So I'm assuming we're picking on Blaine tonight?" Siobhan asked.

Marnel barreled through the other girls and hugged Siobhan quickly before pulling her toward the door. "Yes. Blaine is totally sleeping her way into fancy bars, and I want to know all about it."

Siobhan regarded Marnel with a smirk. "Kind of like we wanted to know about Nate?"

Marnel released Siobhan's arm like she'd suddenly realized it was riddled with gangrene and stormed ahead. "Nope. It's nothing like that at all."

"I'll bet," Siobhan murmured.

They hailed a cab and piled in. Blaine gave the driver the address before the man pulled into traffic without so much as a backward glance. "What's the name of this place?" Siobhan asked.

"The Black Opal," Blaine replied as she pulled a lighted mirror out of her bag and applied a lip balm and bright-red lipstick, and then topped it all off with some type of gloss.

The girls looked at one another skeptically.

"Marnel's right. Who is he?" Siobhan asked.

Blaine looked around, and realizing the question was directed at her, quickly turned off the mirror and threw it in her purse. "What are you talking about?"

"Don't take this the wrong way, because you look stunning, but I highly doubt you're making your lips look that good for us. So who is he?"

"Can't a girl wear a little makeup?"

"A little, yes," Cory answered. "But you basically painted a giant KISS ME sign on your face."

Blaine slumped back in her seat. "You're all ridiculous."

"I'm just getting started," Marnel muttered.

"What was that?" Blaine snapped.

"Oh, nothing."

"I thought we were celebrating Siobhan's gallery opening. Not playing Twenty Questions about my sex life."

Marnel slid closer to Blaine, their faces merely inches apart. "So you're saying you *have* a sex life to talk about?"

"I will head-butt you, so help me God."

"No blood in the cab," the driver yelled.

The girls' heads all snapped in the direction of the driver before they broke out into hysterical laughter that lasted all the way to the bar. They let Blaine lead them up to the entrance, which was indeed guarded by giant bouncers and a velvet rope. She gave her name, and the men nearly tripped over themselves to move the rope for her.

There was definitely a really good story there.

The bar was down a flight of steps into a space that was open and sparsely lit. The female employees were all dressed in various black cabaret costumes while the men wore tight white T-shirts and black fitted pants with suspenders. A jazz band provided the sound track to a place that seemed to have leaped right out of the 1940s. Siobhan's eyes roamed all around as she took in the purple and black striped walls with gold adornments that should have been gaudy but somehow…worked.

This was without a doubt one of the coolest places Siobhan had ever been.

A hostess led them over to a table that already had a bottle of champagne chilling on it. "Bottle service is being provided for you all evening. Please let us know if you require anything else," she said before leaving them slack-jawed at the table.

Marnel slowly panned toward Blaine and just stared at her.

"What?" Blaine finally snapped.

Marnel shook her head. "Do me one favor."

Blaine widened her eyes in annoyance and waited for Marnel to continue.

"Whatever you're doing. Or *whoever*. Keep doing it."

Blaine rolled her eyes before reaching for the bottle of champagne and filling their glasses. When she'd replaced the bottle, she lifted her glass. "Let's toast. To Siobhan. For coming home, and for her exciting new venture."

The girls all clinked glasses and drank the bubbly liquid that went down smoothly.

"So how has it been? Honestly," Cory asked.

Siobhan was confused. "How has what been?"

Cory's face softened. "Having to work at a gallery that ended your relationship."

Siobhan sighed. *So much for celebrating.* "It kinda sucks, to be honest."

"Has he called?"

Siobhan looked at Cory's hopeful yet worried expression. "No."

"I'm surprised," Blaine said. "I thought he'd at least stop by to check on you."

"Why would he?" Siobhan said as she took a long pull of her champagne before setting it down. "He doesn't know I'm back."

Chapter 8

DERICK STARED AT the piece of cardstock in his hand and read it once more. It wasn't that he didn't *want* to see the words written on it; it was just that he couldn't bring himself to fully believe them.

Not only had he received an invitation to the Lost Diamond Gallery's grand opening that would be taking place next month, Siobhan had been the one to invite him. He hadn't even known she was back in New York, let alone planning to run the gallery.

There hadn't been any calls between them since he'd spoken to her about the deed. No texts or emails had been exchanged. He'd been sure that she didn't want to see him. And yet, the invitation in his hand proved otherwise.

But he wasn't exactly sure he wanted to see *her*.

Derick breathed heavily and then tossed the invitation on his counter before grabbing his coat and heading downstairs. He needed to go for a walk to clear his head.

The cool, crisp air hit him in the face as he exited the building. It was exactly what he needed. Maybe the sounds and sights of the city would be enough to get his mind off of her. He rubbed his hands together and blew into them before thrusting them into his pockets and heading down the street.

The movement soothed him, so he walked quickly, crossing streets and turning down others. He'd covered two miles before he'd even realized where he was.

Somehow, in his effort to get away from thoughts of Siobhan and the gallery, he'd ended up right in front of it. It was almost as if his feet had taken him where his mind didn't want to go.

Stopping across the street from the gallery, he looked into the glass exterior, hoping to catch a glimpse of her. Maybe this was best. It didn't matter that they weren't together anymore, that they *wouldn't* be together. He needed to make sure she was okay, happy. He knew his attending the opening was unlikely. What would he even say? *Congratulations on the gallery I bought for you?*

Yup. Voyeurism was definitely way less awkward.

He could see a woman on the phone writing something down, but there was no sign of Siobhan in there. He watched for another few minutes before deciding that he should go home. He took in a deep breath, letting the cool air hit the back of his throat.

And that's when he saw her.

She emerged from the back of the gallery cautiously, her slender fingers wrapped around a painting. She spoke to the other woman for a moment before moving toward the front of the gallery to position the art on an easel in the window display.

Then she pointed toward the side wall and said something else before grabbing some nearby boxes and heading toward the back of the gallery again. She looked so graceful, so confident, so self-assured.

This was where she was supposed to be. Even if he wasn't there with her.

Chapter 9

SIOBHAN LOOKED AROUND the room at the six artists in front of her and tried to not make it apparent how overwhelmed she was. Derick had arranged for all of these artists to show their work at the Lost Diamond, so Siobhan didn't know most of them. Or any of them, really, except for Kayla, because she'd shown with her when Siobhan had first lived in New York.

The artists were buzzing around the gallery, looking at how their work was displayed and perusing the other paintings on the walls. Once the murmur died down, Siobhan decided it was time to get this started.

"If everyone can come this way, I want to run through the schedule for our next couple weeks. Things are going to be very busy before opening night." Siobhan took a few deep breaths as everyone walked toward her and looked at her expectantly. She'd always loved that she could put something on a canvas and have it speak for her. Directing a group of adoring people was way out of her comfort zone.

She ran through the logistics of the evening quickly before asking if anyone had any major changes to the proposals they'd submitted. Other than one artist, who wanted to remove a painting from his exhibit, everyone seemed satisfied.

"Anything else before we head out?" Siobhan asked.

A young abstract painter named Ricardo looked around at the other artists before turning his gaze back on Siobhan. "I wanted to thank you for what you've done here."

Siobhan felt too uncomfortable to accept the praise. "I appreciate that. Though, to be honest, this is my first time doing anything like this. So any insights or suggestions you have, they'd be welcome." Once the words were out, Siobhan realized that she had basically admitted that she was an inexperienced moron flying by the seat of her pants. *Way to instill confidence.*

She was still thinking of a way to take back what she'd said when Ricardo spoke again. "All of us are virtually unknown, so I'm not sure any of us can really offer advice." Laughing a bit, he continued. "I'm just happy for the opportunity to show here. You shouldn't doubt yourself. Mr. Miller was right. You have a great eye. The place looks amazing."

A quick sound of agreement swept through the group.

"Thank you." Siobhan cleared her throat. "That's very kind."

"Is Mr. Miller going to be at the opening?" Sylvia, a small slip of a woman who painted big, bold pieces depicting urban life, asked.

Siobhan's eyes darted toward the ground for a second before answering. "Unfortunately, I don't think he'll be here." Even though she had sent him an invitation, she doubted Derick would actually come. And since she hadn't heard from him, she was sure her doubt was well-founded.

Sylvia's face fell. "Oh. That's such a shame. He seemed so passionate about the gallery."

"Yeah, he was. It was inspirational to hear him talk about it." That had come from Wiley, an untrained artist who drew the human form so well his paintings looked like they were photographs. "I'm surprised that he won't be here. I hope everything's okay."

"He had a prior commitment, I think," Siobhan assured him with a smile that felt too sad to be convincing.

"Must be important if he's missing your opening for it. He clearly thinks the world of you," Wiley said. "He told us how talented and determined you were to pave your own way. He thought other artists could learn from that."

Feeling her eyebrows furrow, Siobhan quickly tried to school her features, not wanting to let on that she evidently knew less about Derick's reasons for opening the gallery than the strangers in this room. "He said all that?" she couldn't help but ask.

"Oh, yeah," Ricardo said. "He said that he saw firsthand how difficult the life of an artist could be, and if he could help relieve even a little bit of that stress that you endured, then he would. But he said that he was just providing the space. It was you who'd make it shine."

"Like a diamond," Sylvia added with a smile.

Siobhan returned the smile, and for the first time in a long time, it didn't feel forced.

Chapter 10

THE DING OF the elevator caused Derick's head to snap up from the paperwork he had been focused on, which was spread out across his dining room table. He rose and moved toward the foyer, wondering who it could be. The doormen never let people up without phoning him first.

He came to an abrupt halt as he saw who was visiting him.

"Hi, Derick." Siobhan's hair was damp from the drizzling rain outside, and she was dressed in a bulky coat to try to stave off the frigid New York air. She was the most beautiful thing he'd ever seen.

"I'm sorry to just drop in. I figured they'd call you before letting me up, but I guess you never told them…umm, told them that…" Siobhan closed her eyes briefly before refocusing on him. "Anyway, when they told me to go up, I figured that, at least this way, you couldn't refuse to see me." She said the last bit with a small laugh, but it sounded strained and awkward.

"I'd never refuse to see you. I'm not a petty teenager holding a grudge." The words came out harsher than he'd intended, but having her here, in his space, was seriously screwing with his head.

Her shoulders slumped a bit at his tone, but she maintained eye contact. "No, I know. I didn't think that. I just…. Okay, I kind of thought that. Mostly because I wouldn't blame you if you didn't want to see me. But maybe that's because *I* typically act like a petty teenager."

She was rambling. And despite the fact that part of him liked that she was nervous—liked that she obviously still cared what he thought about her—another part hurt at the very sight of her. "What are you doing here, Siobhan?"

She chewed her bottom lip for a moment before speaking. "Tell me why you bought the gallery."

Derick couldn't help it. He laughed. "Does it really matter?"

"Yes."

"Why?"

"Because I need to know."

Derick scoffed. "Oh, well, by all means then, let me sit here and recount the whole story. I want nothing more out of life than to give you whatever you need. Never mind what *I* need."

Siobhan lowered her head and stared at the floor. "What do you need, Derick?"

"For you to not ask questions if you aren't interested in hearing the answers to them."

Siobhan's head popped up. "Why wouldn't I be interested? I came all the way here to ask." She sounded exasperated.

"What a hardship. You took a cab a few blocks. I traveled

across *states* for you. I tried to give you everything you needed—
be everything you needed. And for what? So you could punish
me for something you never even gave me the chance to explain?"

She took a step closer to him. "Are you kidding me right now?
You had *months* to explain—to tell me about the gallery. And instead you lied to me."

"I never lied. I was waiting for the right time to tell you."

"Don't give me that. Not telling me is still lying by omission.
Don't draw these fuzzy lines and try to hide the truth between
them. When you didn't tell me that you'd bought a gallery
which you intended for me to run and to display my paintings
in—it was a huge violation of trust."

Derick rubbed his forehead roughly. "Why do you always have
to blow everything out of proportion?"

Siobhan jerked back slightly at that. She took a few deep
breaths, and when she finally responded, her voice was barely
above a whisper. "Why didn't you just tell me?"

"I already answered that. I was waiting for the right time."

"But why was there a right and a wrong time? Come on, Derick. If you hadn't known what you were doing was going to piss
me off, you wouldn't have kept it from me."

Derick shook his head. "What does any of this matter? I say up,
you say down. I go left, you go right. We're never going to see eye
to eye here. The very fact that you think I'd do something that I
knew would hurt you says all that needs to be said. You can't understand where I'm coming from, and I can't understand where

you're coming from. It's that simple, and that tragic, and there's no fixing it."

"I disagree."

Derick huffed out a laugh. "Of course you do."

"Tell me why you bought the gallery."

"Jesus Christ! Because you reminded me what it felt like to watch someone you love struggle and not be able to help them. Or, in your case, not be *allowed* to help them. But when you left, it gave me a broader perspective. You weren't the only one fighting for your dream. So I thought, if I couldn't help you, then maybe I could help them." He had unconsciously moved closer to her, still drawn to her despite his anger.

"I opened the damn place because I love you and admire you. Because I watched you flourish in Detroit. It was like you'd found something there that you couldn't find here and that was bullshit. I can give these people a spot in an empty room, Siobhan, but I can't help them succeed. *You* can. So I put the gallery in your name, and hoped that with time, you'd see yourself how I see you. That you could bring what you found in Detroit back here and share it with these people who desperately need it."

He was right in front of her now. So close he could see the tears collecting in her eyes.

"I don't even know what I found in Detroit anymore," she said, her voice cracking.

She dropped her head, so he put his finger under her chin to tilt her gaze back to him. "I do," he said. "Hope. You found hope there, Siobhan."

And for reasons he couldn't explain other than the fact that her proximity always made him a little stupid, Derick leaned in and pressed his lips to hers. It didn't take long for the kiss to grow more heated. In a moment, they allowed all the emotions that were swirling through them to meet and spark between them like an electrical fire.

He pulled her closer as her lips parted to allow his tongue to sweep over hers. He wanted to consume her. To fold her body into his and keep her with him always.

And it was that thought that made him pull away. Because as much as he wanted to keep her, he didn't trust her to stay.

"We can't do this," he said against her lips, soaking in the last bit of contact. Allowing it to be the closure he needed.

"Can't or won't?" she asked, her eyes searching his.

He dropped his hands and stepped away from her. He shrugged. "Both."

She looked at him for a moment, then nodded. "For what it's worth, I know that I screwed up. I barged in here like I was blaming you, but really, I needed to understand your thinking. I needed to grasp the full scope of how epically I messed everything up. And I'm sorry for that. If I could take it all back—"

"But you can't," he interrupted. "And I'm not trying to be a dick by saying that. It's just the reality. This," he motioned between them and shook his head. "I can't stay on this merry-go-round and expect the scenery to change, you know?"

"But what if it could change?" Her voice was quiet, but he could hear the pleading there.

"It would still only go around in a circle."

She rubbed her hands over her face. "God, that…was a really deep metaphor."

A laugh burst out of him. "Thanks."

She smiled at him, but it was gone quickly. "No. Thank *you*." She gave him a long look before turning to go back to the elevator.

When her back was to him, he couldn't resist imparting one final piece of information. "Do you want to know why I named it the Lost Diamond?"

She turned back to him slowly. "Sure."

"Because even though you lost yourself for a little while there, you still are, and will always be, the toughest, most beautiful person I've ever met."

A few silent tears slipped out then, but she didn't bother to wipe them away. She seemed to be struggling to find words, but the moment really didn't call for any more. They'd said all there was to say.

"Take care of yourself," he finally said, both to end the moment and because he meant it.

She turned and hit the button for the elevator, and the doors slid open immediately. She got on before turning back to him. "Good-bye, Derick."

The doors closed, and she was gone. It was then that he finally said the words and felt the true gravity of them. "Good-bye, Siobhan."

Chapter 11

THAT...IS A really depressing story," Marnel said as she looked at Siobhan with pity in her eyes.

"Tell me about it," Siobhan replied. When she'd asked the girls to go to lunch, she hadn't intended to go into the whole mess, still feeling too raw from it. She'd wanted to be close to people who cared about her. But as soon as they'd arrived, she'd found the whole sordid tale pouring out of her. The release was cathartic. She hadn't realized how much she'd needed it.

"And it only gets worse," she continued.

"For Christ's sake, how could it possibly get worse?" Blaine asked.

Siobhan ignored the implication that her life couldn't get any bleaker. "I need another job," she explained.

"Why? Did that asshole take the gallery back? Because I once dated a hitman who owes me a favor." Marnel's voice was hard and angry. And loud. People at nearby tables all turned to stare.

"Maybe you shouldn't scream that in front of strangers," Cory suggested.

Marnel waved her hand. "Whatever. Their word against mine."

Siobhan was going to argue that it was actually about fifteen words against Marnel's, but decided it was pointless. "No, he didn't take the gallery back. But until it opens and we start selling paintings, there's no money coming in. I need to supplement my income somehow. So it looks like it's back to the want ads for me."

Her friends all looked at one another, smiles spreading across their lips. Then they all trained their eyes back on Siobhan.

"What?" she asked.

Blaine reached across the table and laid her hand on top of Siobhan's. "I think you know what." She gave Siobhan's hand a little pat before withdrawing.

Siobhan was confused for about ten seconds. Then her shoulders drooped and her mouth set in a thin line. "Shit."

Chapter 12

SIOBHAN HAD BEEN back hostessing for a week, and was surprised at how few new faces there were. The restaurant business had always seemed like a pretty transient environment, but the Stone Room had managed to hold on to most of the same staff Siobhan had known when she last worked there. The only notable exception was Hayden, a short, beautiful girl who wanted to be a poet.

The girl seemed reserved, but she'd always been nice when Siobhan had worked with her so far. Siobhan wondered what her story was, but was interrupted by Cory elbowing her. She glared at her friend until Cory tilted her head toward the front of the room.

Siobhan sheepishly turned her attention back to Saul, who was giving her a disapproving look. "I see some things never change," he muttered. "Now that I have your attention, let me repeat myself. We're going to try swapping out our menus for tablets, so keep track of how that's working out and report back to me at the end of your shifts."

"Okay," Siobhan nodded, instantly worrying about how many

tablets she was going to drop before the night was over. What the hell was wrong with giving people regular menus?

Hayden also murmured her assent and Saul disbanded the meeting.

"You really know how to make an impression," Blaine whispered to her as she walked by.

"I'm not *making* one, I'm *maintaining* it," Siobhan replied.

"Very true."

Siobhan and Hayden went to prep the front of the house for opening. It wasn't long before the doors to the Stone Room opened, and Siobhan was forced to carry around expensive electronics and occasionally even pour water in their proximity. It was a nightmare in the making.

"The digital age has gone too far," she grumbled when she returned to the hostess station after dropping a tablet in some guy's lap. If his Lamaze-like breathing was any indication, she'd made contact with a very sensitive part of his anatomy.

"What happened?" Hayden asked.

"Oh, nothing. I just castrated a customer. No big deal."

A cackle burst out of Hayden, and Siobhan realized it was the first time she'd heard the other hostess laugh.

Siobhan tried, and failed, to hide her smile. "I'm glad you find it so amusing."

Hayden wiped tears from her eyes. "I really do. God, I haven't laughed like that in a long time."

"Well, pay attention because I'm sure that's not the worst thing that will happen to me tonight."

Hayden chuckled lightly again. "I'm not sure it can get much worse than that." She then turned her attention to a customer who'd walked in. "Though I guess I better seat this one. He's too good-looking for you to harm."

Siobhan smiled and looked over her shoulder to see who Hayden was referring to.

And as Hayden welcomed the guest, Siobhan felt her heart drop. The night was definitely about to get worse.

Chapter 13

DERICK HONESTLY DIDN'T know what the hell he was doing at the Stone Room. Well, he did, but he still wasn't sure why he'd *let* it happen.

When his buddy Jack had called and asked Derick to meet him there for drinks, Derick had initially balked. He'd heard Siobhan was back working there, and he knew that they both needed a clean break. But when his friend had started busting his balls about avoiding his favorite hangout because of a breakup, Derick had caved. The man's logic had made sense on the phone.

It made no sense now.

Because even though Derick didn't want to disrupt his life due to a breakup, what had happened with Siobhan was more than that. It was a shattering.

Not helping matters was the fact that Siobhan was actively avoiding him. She kept her eyes focused directly in front of her whenever she walked past his table. Not to mention that she was as rigid as a flagpole.

Even though he'd convinced himself on the way over that he

and Siobhan were adults who were capable of inhabiting the same room without it being amazingly awkward, he really should have known better. Because as Siobhan tried to look anywhere but at Derick, Derick had a difficult time looking anywhere except at her. He tried to be stealthy about it, casting glances over his glass as he took long gulps of his drink, and constantly adjusting his position so that he'd have a reason to twist in her direction.

It really sucked, he realized, to be so pathetic.

Chapter 14

FORTY-FIVE MINUTES. That's how long Derick lasted before he had to get the hell out of there. He was clearly affecting Siobhan's job performance, since he was pretty sure it was a bad idea for her to ignore an entire section of the club.

And also, he felt...sad. It was too difficult to look at the one thing he wanted most in the world all the while knowing he couldn't have it. So he pulled his coat tightly around him and stepped out onto the sidewalk, turning toward home. He needed to walk a little, try to shake off some of the melancholy that had settled into his bones.

He made it about twenty feet before he heard someone calling his name behind him. Derick knew the voice, and his body instinctively turned toward it before his brain could catch up. He waited for her to reach him, and when she did, he saw the hard set of her features, and braced himself. The cold air whipped all around him.

"What the hell are you doing here?" she asked.

He narrowed his eyes. "What? I can't meet a friend for drinks?"

She rolled her eyes. "You had to do that here? There was nowhere else in the entire city that you guys could have gone?"

Crossing his arms over his chest, he glared down at her. "Why should I rearrange my plans? I've been coming here for years. I shouldn't have to change my whole life around to accommodate you."

Some of the fight seemed to drain out of her. "Why are you doing this to me, Derick?"

He allowed his arms to fall to his sides. "What do you mean?"

"I get that I was horrible to you. I get that I was wrong. But believe me, you telling me good-bye was punishment enough. You don't need to keep reminding me of what I lost. It's already something I'll never be able to forget."

He let out a deep breath, causing white air to puff out in front of him. "I'm not trying to make things harder for you, Siobhan." But as he said the words, he wasn't so sure they were true. He knew she was right. He could have told Jack to meet him somewhere else. Some casual ribbing from one of his friends had never pressured him into doing anything before. But it had tonight—because he'd let it.

Derick had wanted to see her. But more than that, he'd wanted to *be* seen by her. Had wanted her to have to watch him doing something normal and ordinary, as if his life had gone back to how it had been before her.

As if he could even remember what that life had been like.

The realization made his chest ache. He'd told her that he'd never want to hurt her intentionally.

Maybe he was a liar after all.

"It won't happen again," he said, peering into her eyes and hoping that she could see he meant it.

She sniffled a little, her eyes darting around the busy street. "Good," she said. "You wanted this to be over, Derick. I need you to follow through with it. It'll be hard enough trying to get over you without having to see you all the time."

She turned to go but his hand reached out before she could move away from him. He didn't want to look back on this moment and know that he hadn't been honest during it. That he hadn't been the man he'd always claimed to be. He'd already lost too much to also lose himself.

"I don't want you to get over me."

Siobhan looked up at him. "What?"

He stepped closer to her. "I don't want you to get over me. Because I'll never get over you."

And without knowing who made the first move, Derick and Siobhan were kissing in the middle of a busy Manhattan street, displaying a love that would never die but seemed to manage to always destroy them both.

Chapter 15

SIOBHAN FELL BACK against Derick's bed, his weight pressing against her as his lips moved wildly over her skin. She allowed herself to let go, to submit to what they both knew would always be a constant between them. No matter how much one might push the other away, the pull back to each other was a stronger force than anything else in their lives.

"God, I've missed you," she breathed into his ear before sliding her teeth over it.

Derick's response was a low groan that reverberated down her spine as his erection ground against her through his jeans.

"You're so hard," she said. "I want you."

"Yeah?"

She could feel him smile against her throat as he spoke.

"Mm-hmm," she answered.

The coarse hair of his beard tickled as his mouth moved lower—down to her collarbone and over her stomach as he lifted her shirt over her head. She wanted his hands all over her.

His knees straddled her as he sat up on her thighs, pinning her in a place she didn't want to move from anyway. She could see his cock straining against his pants. Needing to feel it, she ran her hands over his length through the denim before unbuttoning his jeans and yanking the zipper down. "Mmm," she moaned as she rubbed her hand over him through the bright-white cotton of his tight boxer briefs.

Derick jerked his hips a bit at her touch and then moved to the side to guide her onto her stomach. He unhooked her bra and slid it over each arm so she could shimmy out of it.

She already loved this—her face pressing against Derick's bed so she could inhale his scent. God, she'd even missed *that*.

His fingers ran along her spine and over the sensitive flesh of her shoulder blades and the back of her neck. She was already grinding against the bed, needing any sort of friction she could get to soothe the sweet ache between her thighs. She knew how wet she must be and could feel the slickness that had probably been there since she'd first seen him at the bar. She didn't even need him to touch her. His proximity to her was an aphrodisiac on its own.

And now here she was, lying in his bed again as he touched the most intimate parts of her. He'd been toying with her thong, pulling away the lace far enough to stroke his finger slowly around her entrance without pushing inside. It was a blissful torture that only he knew how to provide.

Finally Derick pulled her thong down from under her skirt and pushed his fingers inside her. "That feel good?" he asked when she bucked against the mattress.

"God, yeah," she said, the comforter stifling her voice as she reached up to grab the edge of the bed so she could ride Derick's fingers. She was already so close to coming, her body tensing with every smooth motion of his hand, every stroke of his fingertips inside her as they pressed against her walls. "I have no idea what you're doing, but don't stop doing it."

Derick released a small laugh. "I wasn't planning on it," he said, sliding his finger between her ass cheeks.

And that's when she came undone. Her hips jerked wildly over his hand as the waves of her release coursed through her, undulating down her core until they gradually subsided.

"God, you're sexy when you come," Derick said.

He pulled his hand away, leaving her feeling empty and wanting again. She raised her ass in the air enough for him to hike her tight black skirt up around her hips. "I want you, Derick."

"Yeah?" he asked, his hand massaging the cheek of her ass before smacking his palm hard against it. "How do you want it?"

She nearly yelped at the contact. "Jesus, do that again," she pleaded.

Thankfully he complied, his hand striking her already sensitive skin with a sharp crack. Then she felt the head of Derick's cock between her thighs, rubbing delicately over her clit. The slickness from her orgasm lubricated him as he slipped against her, holding himself in his hand as he moved his dick between her folds.

Desperate to have him inside her, she wiggled against him. "Please, Derick. Make me come again."

"Like this? Is this what you want?"

"Yes," she huffed.

And that's when Derick thrust inside her, plunging so deep it felt like he might stay a part of her forever.

Maybe he would.

The fullness she felt as he retracted and then slammed into her had her nearly losing it again. But she wanted to wait for him to get there, too, to feel the pressure building inside her until she was ready to burst.

His movements grew faster, more forceful. And she could tell he was getting close.

God, she wanted him to come, to get lost in her as he let go.

"Come. God, now," he said as he reached around to stroke her clit in a way that had her coming almost instantly.

She could feel Derick straining, and she knew he was trying to hold off as he stroked her through the lingering pulses of her orgasm.

But as soon as she was done, he pulled out of her, flipping her over again so she could see his hand stroking his cock furiously as he raced toward his own release. She'd never watched him do this to himself before, and it might have been the sexiest thing she'd ever seen.

She took all of him in—the flexed muscles of his chest and shoulders, the hard lines of his abs. Then his entire body tensed with pleasure and he came.

She hadn't expected to love it as much as she did. But the way he'd taken control of her, marked her, had her wondering why they hadn't done this before now.

Derick leaned down and pressed a lingering kiss to her lips before standing and heading to the bathroom. He returned with a warm washcloth and wiped himself from her body. Once she was clean, he tossed the washcloth into the hamper before returning to the bed and sliding in beside her. He wrapped his arm around her, pulling her close.

Pressing his face into her hair, he inhaled deeply.

Siobhan wasn't sure what to make of his silence. He seemed content wrapping himself around her in his bed, but she was afraid to hope. Settling back into him, she decided that words could wait for morning.

Chapter 16

SOFT SUNLIGHT STREAMED through the window, casting pale light over Siobhan as she slept beside him.

He could feel the rise and fall of her chest against his as her head rested in the crook of his arm. Derick wanted to exist in this moment forever. Everything was uncomplicated as they lay there, snuggled together.

But the reality was pretty damn complicated.

It had been easy for Derick to ignore their issues in the rush of passion that overtook them as they had stood there in the darkness. Issues that couldn't be ignored in the stark light of day.

Derick shook Siobhan lightly. "Hey," he whispered into her temple when she'd roused. "I think we need to talk."

Chapter 17

SIOBHAN FELT LIKE she was moving on autopilot as she scooted up the bed to lean back against Derick's oversized plush pillow, pulling the sheet over herself as she went. Derick's tone let her know that what was coming was probably something she didn't want to be naked for.

He sat down on the edge of the bed and turned toward her. He watched his hands as they twisted in his lap before he took a deep breath and looked at her.

She wasn't sure what she saw in his eyes. Uncertainty? Sadness? Relief? She wanted to ask, but Derick had requested this conversation. She'd let him lead it.

Finally he cleared his throat in a way that let her know he was slightly uncomfortable. "That was...Christ, what is wrong with us?"

Her eyes widened. Hearing him imply that what they had just shared was wrong somehow was shocking. And painful. She hoped that he hadn't meant it the way it sounded. "That's a long list," she said with an awkward laugh that she prayed covered how badly his words had stung her.

Derick rubbed his face with his hands. "I'm sorry, Siobhan."

"Me, too. I know I've already said it, but Derick, I really am so sorry. I've punished you for my own issues and insecurities, but I'm done with that. Done hurting us both. You're a great man, and I've been crazy to not accept you for who you are. We just need to—"

"No, that's not…" Derick stood abruptly and stalked away from her a few steps before turning around. "God, I messed this up so badly." He returned to his spot on the bed and looked at her intently. "You say you're sorry, and I can forgive you, Siobhan. I really can. Neither of us has been innocent in all of this. But when it comes to forgetting it…" Derick shook his head. "That's something I can't do."

Siobhan felt her entire body seize as though all the oxygen had been suddenly removed from the room. "What…what are you saying?"

"We can't do this. Come on, Siobhan. You know we can't. How many times have we been in this exact place? How many times do we have to hurt each other before we leave well enough alone?" Derick's face softened. "I know I said I didn't want you to get over me. And that's the truth. But that doesn't mean that I don't think you should. That we *both* should."

Despite racking her brain for words, Siobhan kept coming up empty. After a few tense and silent moments, she quickly got up from the bed and started dressing.

Derick remained silent as she pulled her clothes on. The only sound was the opening of a drawer and the rustling of his putting clothes on, too.

She didn't turn and look at him once she finished dressing. Instead, she made her way out of his bedroom in search of the shoes she'd kicked off somewhere last night. Tears were prickling behind her eyes, but she'd be damned if she'd lose that bit of dignity, too. She would not let him see her cry. Once she'd put her heels on, she made her way toward the elevator.

"Wait, Siobhan…don't…don't leave like this."

She turned around and gave a dry laugh. "Like what, exactly?" Her eyes grazed over Derick in sweatpants and a tight black T-shirt. It struck her that this was probably the last time she'd ever see him dressed this casually. Maybe the last time she'd ever see him *period*.

He sighed heavily, his shoulders slumping with the exhale. "Hating me."

Siobhan's eyes fell to the floor to try and keep the tears at bay. Once she felt more in control, she looked back up. "I don't hate you, Derick."

He scoffed. "Really? Because I hate me right now. Bringing you back here…it was weak of me. I'm sorry I'm such an asshole."

Shrugging, she offered him the last bit of truth she had. "It's not like you dragged me here. We both made decisions—today, yesterday, and all the days before."

"We both did make some pretty epic mistakes."

Siobhan shook her head. "That's where you're wrong, Derick. Nothing between us was ever a mistake."

He didn't respond to that, and she really didn't want him to. She managed to keep the tears from falling through the elevator ride and the walk out of his building. But as her feet hit the side-walk, the dam broke.

Siobhan had always been able to pick herself up no matter how difficult the circumstances were, but this time, she truly didn't know if she'd be able to get past what she'd cost herself. Because ultimately, how valuable was a lost diamond when the one who had treasured it most didn't want it anymore?

Chapter 18

GOD, THAT'S SO depressing," Marnel said, putting her lemon water back down on the table.

Siobhan glared at her as she pushed her hands through her hair and rested her head between them. "Can you please stop saying that?"

Marnel shrugged. "I call it like I see it. Start telling some stories that are a little more uplifting and maybe you'll get a different response."

Cory elbowed her. "Show some compassion."

"So I'm confused," Blaine said. "It *wasn't* make-up sex?"

Siobhan huffed and pushed off of her elbows. "No. It was probably more like…" She shook her head as she searched it for an accurate description. "Like 'I can't help myself even though I know this is a terrible idea' sex."

"It's not," Cory said. "He wants you. He wouldn't have had sex with you if he didn't. He just doesn't *want* to want you. And he probably doesn't believe you'll love him unconditionally. Every time he does something too over-the-top you reject him. Then he has to come crawling back. All that groveling probably gets tiring, not to mention somewhat emasculating," she added.

"Thanks for that," Siobhan deadpanned. "That makes me feel more awesome than I already do," she said.

"Seriously, though," Cory continued. "You've said all this before. There's gotta come a point when he stops believing it."

"Yeah," Marnel said. "Actions speak louder than words and all that. You gotta *show* him that you're willing to accept him completely."

Siobhan looked to the other girls, who seemed to agree. "What am I supposed to do?" she asked.

"I don't know," Marnel said. "But you need to do *some*thing. Otherwise your relationship is gonna keep playing out like that Justin Bieber song." Marnel smiled, clearly pleased with the connection she'd made. "It's too late now to say you're sorry, Siobhan. Speaking of that, pretty soon Saul's not going to accept your sorrys either. I can't believe he bought that you were sick when you ran out of there the other night. Wait…did you have, what did you call it? 'I can't help myself even though this is a horrible idea sex' with Saul, too?"

Siobhan stared at her silently for a few seconds before she spoke. "I despise you," she said, causing all of the girls to erupt in a fit of laughter.

Marnel cocked her head to the side, looking confused. "You *love* me."

And Siobhan couldn't help but smile. She really did.

Chapter 19

DERICK COULDN'T BELIEVE what he was looking at. This was the worst déjà vu he'd ever experienced. He brushed his thumb over the cardstock, unable to stop staring at the invitation he'd just received for the Lost Diamond. *Why would she send another one?*

Shaking his head, he flicked the invitation toward the table. It missed and fell to the ground, which caused him to see writing on the back. He snatched it back up and read the neatly printed words.

You've given me so many declarations of your love, I lost count of all of them. Allow me to return the favor, even if it's just this once. You don't owe it to me to come, but I hope you will anyway.

Love always,
Siobhan

Derick walked to the couch and dropped onto it, the invitation still in his hands. He reread the message over and over again. When he'd finally had enough, he was left with only one question. What the hell was he supposed to do now?

Chapter 20

THE PREVIOUS THREE weeks had been the busiest of Siobhan's life, but as she stood back and looked over the crowd that had packed into the Lost Diamond, she knew it had all been worth it.

The sound of Kayla's voice startled her. "Siobhan," she said, her voice light and singsongy.

Siobhan looked over her shoulder to see Kayla nearly bouncing with joy. Siobhan hadn't even thought it was possible to jump that high in five-inch heels. "Yes," she sang back, somehow dragging out the word into multiple syllables.

"Whatcha up to?"

"I was…having a moment, I guess you could say." She still couldn't believe this night was actually happening.

Kayla threw her arm around Siobhan excitedly. "Well, I'm interrupting your moment to give you an update."

Siobhan raised her eyebrows. "An update?"

"Yeah. Ricardo just sold his first painting. Like ever. And he's flipping out right now."

"Really? That's fantastic!" She remembered what that felt like—for someone else to think you're talented, worthy. Unfortunately, that memory brought up another, less pleasant one. But as quickly as it popped into her head, she dismissed it. She only wanted happiness for Ricardo. "I need to go congratulate him," she said, peering around the crowd to see him speaking to someone and grinning widely.

"You can do that later," Kayla replied, grabbing onto Siobhan's bicep and spinning her in the other direction. "You see that guy over there? The one in the dark-gray suit?"

"There are like three guys in dark-gray suits. Who am I looking at?"

"Gray hair. Two o'clock," Kayla said. "But don't make it obvious that you're looking at him."

"You just *told* me to look at him."

Kayla shook her head and sighed. "Yeah, look. But don't make it obvious. That's Stephen Ramsey."

Siobhan's eyes widened so far she thought they might pop out of her head. "Holy shit! I didn't even see him come in." What the hell was one of the city's well-known art critics doing at her small gallery opening?

"At first, I didn't see him, either. I just noticed him a few minutes ago. The woman he's with must be another critic. I heard them talking, and they love your work. You should go introduce yourself."

"What should I say?"

"Your name's a good start."

"*Annnd* then I'll just stare awkwardly until the silence gets so uncomfortable that they walk away."

"That's probably not a good tactic," Kayla said.

"Thanks. I figured." Siobhan picked up a glass of champagne from a nearby tray. "I need a drink. And I need something to do with my hands. I never know what to do with them when I talk to people." She downed about half the glass and turned toward Kayla. "Okay, okay, okay," she said quickly. "I'm going over. Wish me luck."

Kayla put her hands on Siobhan's arms and looked her in the eyes. "Good luck," she said, taking note of Siobhan's free hand that was rubbing itself nervously. "You're gonna need it. You really *are* awkward as hell."

"Not helping," Siobhan joked, before turning toward the critics and plastering on what she hoped was a confident and relaxed smile.

She extended her hand as she approached. "Mr. Ramsey, thank you so much for coming. I'm Siobhan Dempsey, the owner of the Lost Diamond."

Mr. Ramsey smiled and shook her hand firmly. "Siobhan, lovely to meet you. Please call me Stephen." He gestured around the room. "You've done a wonderful job with your gallery. Allow me to introduce you to my colleagues."

Once they'd gone through the introductions, Siobhan felt like she was going to levitate with a mixture of excitement and anxiety.

"We saw your pieces. I must say, I haven't seen paintings with that much emotion packed into a canvas in a long time."

Siobhan tried not to blush at Stephen's compliment. "Thank you. It's been…a labor of love."

Stephen and the other critics nodded. "I hope you don't mind if I find you in a bit and ask for a quote to put with my review."

"Of course." Siobhan laughed in an attempt to hide the fact that she'd nearly swallowed her tongue at his words.

Stephen patted her on the arm. "Good. You are quite gifted, Siobhan. New York is lucky to have you back."

Siobhan watched the group drift away, stunned not only by the fact that Stephen liked her work but also that he was aware that she had left the city and then returned.

During the next couple of hours, people continued to congratulate her and the other artists. And a few more paintings sold.

All in all, the night was turning out to be a huge success.

Yet there was one thing missing.

"Has he shown up yet?" Cory asked as she sidled up to Siobhan and handed her a glass of champagne, which Siobhan happily took.

"No."

Cory bumped Siobhan's shoulder softly. "He will."

Siobhan smiled gratefully at her friend. "No. He probably won't." She reached out to squeeze Cory's shoulder, thankful for the support, before leaving to mingle.

As she talked with her guests, Siobhan realized that she'd gotten exactly what she deserved. She'd spent three weeks putting her "grand gesture" together. It was fitting that Derick would never see it, since she'd never let him show her any of his grand gestures, either.

Chapter 21

DERICK REALLY DIDN'T know what the hell he was doing at the gallery. He'd talked himself out of going at least fifteen times. Yet here he was, succumbing to his own stupid curiosity even though it would likely cost him his sanity.

He scanned the crowd, but didn't see Siobhan. He wasn't sure if he was happy or sad at that.

"What you're looking for is in the back."

Derick whirled around toward the voice and saw Marnel standing behind him, a gentle smile on her lips. He sighed and said, "I'm not sure what I'm even looking for."

"Then I guess you'll have to have faith that I do."

She was gone before he could reply, and Derick found himself moving toward the back of the gallery. The first thing he saw was Siobhan's name written in bold black letters on the wall above a series of paintings that spanned the entire rear wall.

Why would Marnel send him back here? He'd already seen these paintings—had already had enough problems caused by them.

But when he actually looked at the art on the wall, he realized that the paintings hanging in front of him weren't the ones he'd bought. "What the hell," he whispered to himself.

He started by looking at the painting on the far left, which he guessed was meant to be viewed first. He was right. It was a picture of a man catching a girl before she fell. The background colors were muted and streaked, allowing the brightness and stillness of the two figures to stand out in stark contrast to the life that kept moving on around them. The figures gazed at each other, time stopping for them even though the rest of the world was a blur of color. Derick's eyes flicked to the placard beside it, and he read the title: *Fated to Fall.*

Moving to the next one, he saw a man holding court among a flock of old ladies. They were all smiling as they sat beside their easels. Everyone was engaged except for one figure—a young woman standing slightly apart, wearing a small smile on her face as she watched the scene unfold. *A Central Focus.*

Derick kept moving through the paintings, watching his and Siobhan's love story unfold before him. Every major moment between them was accounted for. Their tour to the top of the Empire State Building—*Penny Wishes;* their lunch at Burger Joint—*Hidden Truths;* their rooftop dinner at the Met with the fireworks in the background—*Illumination of Love.*

Then he came to one that stopped him short. He and Siobhan were in it, but they were surrounded by vibrant colors. Pictures swirled around them—elements of the paintings Derick had bought. The woman was holding her hands out, handing the man something. Derick had to move closer to see what it was, and his breath caught when he finally saw it. Her heart.

His eyes looked frantically for the title: *Lost to You.*

Part of him didn't want to see any more, but he knew he had to see it through. She'd painted herself looking into a window and seeing his reflection. The next depicted Derick's arm wrapped around her as they stood on the shore of Belle Isle. Another showed him wrapping a robe around her as a group of painters looked on.

Then he arrived at the one he knew would be there but had hoped wasn't. It was a painting of the gallery. Derick was to the far right, barely on the canvas. His arm was outstretched toward Siobhan, but her back was to him as she entered the building. The title was self-explanatory: *The Lost Diamond.*

The next one was unlike any of the others. It was a riot of colors and seemed almost abstract until he looked at it more closely. That's when he made out the naked limbs among the swirling mixture of paints and textures. Derick still wasn't sure what he was seeing until he looked at the title: *Chaotic Passion.*

It was their last time together, the encounter Derick had callously called a mistake. He wasn't sure if he was interpreting the painting correctly or not, but as he looked at the two figures, it felt as if they were almost completely concealed by layers of paint and color.

Because, ultimately, he and Siobhan had allowed themselves to be obscured by all the emotions they'd carried since the beginning, hadn't they? How could their relationship ever have stood a chance when it was blanketed by the chaos of the burdens and re-sentments and pain they'd both collected along the way?

It took a jumble of paint on a canvas for him to finally see things clearly.

Derick looked to his right where the last canvas rested. But this one—titled *The Future*—was blank.

"I wasn't sure what to put there yet."

Derick didn't bother to turn around. He knew who had spoken.

"Me neither," he replied.

Chapter 22

SIOBHAN COULD ONLY manage shallow breaths as her heart expanded and took up all the available room in her chest. She tried to read his body language, but with his tailored suit and his back to her, she couldn't get any sense of how he felt.

He had sounded genuinely unsure. But, against her better judgment, she let a shred of hope seep into her. Because if he didn't know what the future held for him, maybe there was a chance that Siobhan could still be part of it.

He rubbed a hand over his beard as he continued to stare at her paintings. "Seeing all this, laid out like this…it's hard to believe we've known each other for less than a year. This is a lot to have gone through."

Siobhan nodded even though he couldn't see her. The truth was, despite the fact that she'd created the paintings for Derick, a part of her had thought he would never actually get to see them. "I think the depth of our feelings for each other came on so quickly that we condensed years of relationship-building into months."

Letting out a short laugh, Derick turned his head slightly and flicked his eyes in her direction before facing the wall again. "We've definitely put each other through the wringer."

Not being able to stand the distance any longer, Siobhan moved next to him. "Yeah, we have. But it was funny. When I was conceptualizing all of this, I felt like the bad moments would be where I'd feel the most emotion. That reliving them would be the most painful." She turned and looked at him. "But they weren't." She gestured down toward the first few paintings. "The good memories were the hardest to paint because I knew I might never experience any more of them."

"Listen, Siobhan, I get—"

But she lifted a hand to stop him. What she was saying wasn't an excuse or a plea. It was merely a simple truth she'd uncovered as she'd painted their story. And she needed to share it with him before any other words were said. "When we fight, we fight hard." She shrugged. "We're passionate people, Derick. We're opinionated, stubborn, and, at times, downright infuriating."

He let out a soft chuckle at her description.

She grabbed the fabric covering his bicep and tugged until he turned to face her fully. "But we're also dedicated. To our careers, to carving out the best life possible for ourselves, and—whether we like it or not—to each other."

Derick's eyes drifted away from hers but he didn't dispute what she'd said.

Siobhan pointed at the blank canvas. "If you can look at that—if you can think about your future—and see someone else there, then I'll walk away right now and never bother you again. But I need you to know that I can't imagine anyone else in that picture with me. And I really don't want that"—she gestured to the painting of the disconnected limbs lost in the fray of color—"to be how we end."

She stepped in front of him, partially obstructing his view of the art on the wall. Cutting off his gaze from what was, and hopefully directing it on what could be. "I know that I've told you that I'll accept you as you are so many times and I haven't. So I started painting this exhibit to show you that words aren't enough for me to show you how I feel. I'm capable of more than that. I know that everything you've ever done for me has been because you loved me and wanted to support me. And for once, I wanted to accept your gift and show that I was grateful for it. You bought me a gallery to show me your love." Siobhan turned her head briefly to the paintings behind her. "And I filled it with paintings of how that love came to be.

"As I painted, I realized that our love might not be easy or convenient or perfect. But it's ours. We created it together. I don't want to scrap it just because it's not always as pretty as we initially pictured it to be."

And there it was, everything Siobhan felt in her heart splayed out for him. He could do whatever he wanted with it. As vulnerable as it made her, Siobhan had never felt freer. At least if he walked away, he would walk away knowing exactly where she stood.

They stood in silence for a few moments. Derick's eyes darted from Siobhan to the paintings and back to Siobhan. "God, I don't…this is so…I'm really overwhelmed."

Siobhan nodded and took a small step back to give him the space he obviously needed. "Tell you what. Tomorrow around noon I'm going to go up the Empire State Building and make one final wish. If you decide…" Her voice started to break, so she cleared her throat. "If you think of anything you'd like to wish for, then you can meet me there. And if not…" She allowed a shrug to speak the words she didn't think she'd be able to get out.

Derick ran a hand through his hair as he gave the paintings one last look. Then he turned to her and nodded.

Smiling softly, Siobhan turned to go back to her guests.

"Siobhan?"

"Yeah?"

"No matter where you thought life would take you, you were meant to end up here in this gallery. Only you could've breathed this kind of life into it."

"I know," she replied softly, finally accepting what he offered.

Chapter 23

DERICK NEEDED TO get away from the gallery, away from Siobhan, and away from...everything. The frigid night air was abrasive, but Derick was trying to feel anything other than raw.

Derick's hand reached into his pocket to grab his phone. He'd told his driver to circle the block until he received Derick's call. But the thought of being cooped up in a confined space—even if that space was fairly large—made Derick's skin crawl. He needed to be out in the open where he could take deep, clear breaths and process everything that had just happened.

He put the call through, let the driver know he was going to walk, and hung up as he heard the driver asking if he was sure.

Because Derick wasn't sure of anything anymore.

But then he realized that that wasn't totally true. He was sure that breaking things off with Siobhan had been the right move. Yeah, it hurt like hell, and he felt a loss akin to losing a limb—or at least what Derick thought such a loss would feel like—but that didn't make it wrong. Look at all Siobhan had accomplished since he'd left her alone. She was flourishing, and he would, too. Eventually. He was pretty sure.

Derick didn't want to go home to his empty apartment, but the streets were crowded and bustling, and he couldn't stand it anymore. So when he came upon a movie theater, Derick went in and walked up to the counter. "One adult, please."

"Uh, for which movie, sir?"

Derick scanned the movie titles listed behind the kid at the counter. "Which one is beginning next?"

"*A Savior in Blue* just started."

Derick had vaguely recognized it. He was pretty sure it was an action movie. "Sounds good." Derick paid and was given his ticket in return. "Thanks," he said before making his way into the theater.

He went directly into the movie and found a seat near the front. The opening credits were still playing, and Derick settled back into his seat, hoping to get lost in the plot to give his mind a brief reprieve from the disaster that was his relationship with Siobhan.

Who did she think she was, anyway, painting all of those pieces and forcing him to take a trip down memory lane? Did she really think he needed the reminder of the time they spent together? Because he didn't. There was nothing about Siobhan he'd forgotten. He was worried he'd never forget.

As the movie began, he glanced around him. He was surrounded by couples. *Figures*. But as he slumped back in his seat, he realized that he and Siobhan had never been one of these couples. How was it possible that after all they'd been through, they'd never gone to a movie together?

The thought made the cloud of irritation that had been hovering over him burst into a downpour of sadness. He'd always been focused on making things special, bordering on over-the-top, even though it often made Siobhan uncomfortable. Sitting in a dark theater holding hands would have been enough for her.

Derick felt a profound sense of loss at all of the simple moments they had never shared. The ones they never would share, unless he made a different choice. All this time, he'd been so sure of what he was giving up by walking away. The clenching in his chest told him he hadn't even begun to imagine it.

Staring at the screen, Derick tried to force his brain to focus on the movie. By about the halfway point, he congratulated himself on being moderately successful. Unfortunately, that was when the main character—who was a police officer—started to fall in love with the woman he was protecting.

As the movie continued, and the on-screen relationship grew steamier, Derick began to fidget. Obviously, there was no parallel between what he'd had with Siobhan and what was playing out on the screen, especially since he was pretty sure Siobhan had never been hunted by the mob. But watching something real—or fictionally real—develop between two people who appeared to be opposites…it was overwhelming. Which was why Derick found himself getting up and exiting the theater before the movie ended. He wasn't up for the happily-ever-after moment.

Once outside, he hailed a cab and gave his address. He barely remembered the ride, his mind a chaotic jumble of scenarios, consequences, and truths. When he arrived at his building, he paid the fare and hurried up to his apartment.

Staring out at the New York skyline lit up in the dark and starless night, Derick laid it all out to himself. Siobhan had poured her heart out to him in her paintings. He knew that. But how many times had he done the same, only to be cut off by her? He loved her—God, did he love her—but was that enough?

He'd wished for so many things since he met her, and he hadn't been granted any of them. Could he go to the top of the Empire State Building the next day and make another, knowing the outcome would likely be the same?

He just didn't know.

Eventually he threw himself into bed and fell into a fitful sleep. The next morning, he stood in his closet wondering what kind of day he should be dressing for. He was no closer to knowing what to do than he had been the night before. His heart said one thing while his brain told him another. It was torture.

He looked down at his watch. It was quarter after eleven, and if he didn't make up his mind soon, he'd lose the ability to even make a choice.

Screw it. Sometimes, when his brain and heart couldn't get on the same page, Derick had to rely on his gut instinct. And as he walked out of his closet, he hoped his instincts wouldn't fail him when he needed them most.

Chapter 24

THE DISPLAY ON her phone showed the time: twelve thirty. There was her answer. He really wasn't coming.

Siobhan gripped the fence surrounding the observation deck and leaned into it, breathing in the cold air and willing it to numb her insides. "So that's it then," she whispered to herself as if the words could convince her heart to stop aching.

She pushed her hand into her coat pocket and pulled out the penny she'd put there that morning. As she stared at it, she silently talked herself out of making the obvious wish: that he would still show up and take her back. It was abundantly clear that that wasn't happening so to wish for it would be a waste. This was the last wish she ever intended to make, after all. She had to make it good.

Finally, it came to her. And as a single tear streaked down her cheek, she said the wish aloud to give it flight. "Be happy, Derick." She placed the penny onto the ledge, and then took a small step back, crossing her arms over her chest and staring out at the city.

She felt someone move next to her, so she scooted over to make room for them. Her eyes caught movement beside her as a hand reached out toward her penny. Just as she was about to yell at the stranger not to touch it, she saw the hand drop a penny right beside hers.

Her head whipped around toward the stranger. Or the man she thought was a stranger. She felt her eyes widen as her lips parted.

"Thank goodness you can never be too late to make a wish. Otherwise I'd have missed my chance," Derick said.

Siobhan bit her lower lip and willed the tears not to fall. "What did you wish for?" she asked, emotion making her voice low and gravelly.

Derick turned toward her and pulled her to him. His smile was wide. "To kiss you on top of the Empire State Building."

She couldn't help the chuckle that escaped her. "You wished for that last time."

"What can I say? I believe in sticking with what works." And with that, he leaned down and pressed his lips to hers.

Neither of them moved to deepen the kiss. The steady contact was all they needed in that moment. It was more than Siobhan had ever hoped to experience again.

When Derick pulled back, he rested his forehead against hers. "What was your wish?"

Siobhan nuzzled closer to him for a second. For some reason, she was slightly embarrassed to tell him her wish. But after a couple of seconds of contemplation, she pulled back so she could look him in the eyes, and said, "For you to be happy."

Chapter 25

DERICK COULDN'T KEEP his hands off of Siobhan. He gave it a valiant effort since they were, after all, in public. But his self-control—which had never been anything to brag about—was crumbling.

He hadn't wanted to rush Siobhan back to his place. The last time they'd done that was a less-than-happy memory for them, and he wanted to do better this time. *Be* better. So he'd suggested grabbing lunch, to which Siobhan had happily agreed.

It had started with a hand on her back as they got on the crowded elevator. Then it progressed to him pulling her body flush against his front—to make more room, of course—as they rode down. He was going to reach for her hand when they made their way onto the sidewalk, but that wasn't enough contact, so he wrapped an arm around her shoulders instead.

They walked to a small café on the corner and were seated fairly quickly, considering it was the lunch rush. As Derick sat across from her, he couldn't help but be amazed by the fact that they were there together. It had all come down to the one fact that he knew

Derick smiled brightly. "Guess we both got what we wished for then."

And as Siobhan wound her arms around Derick's neck, she knew that actually, they'd gotten something more.

was indisputable: he would never love anyone the way he loved Siobhan.

And despite the doubts he'd still had during his trip to the Empire State Building, once he'd gotten there, the tension had immediately drained from him. It was like his body instinctively knew what his mind had been struggling to accept.

"Derick?"

Siobhan's voice snapped him out of his thoughts. "Yeah?"

"Would you like to order a drink from this nice woman?" Siobhan smirked at him.

It made him want to kiss her. "Uh, sure, um, I'll have a water for now."

The server smiled and left their table, which made Derick realize Siobhan must have already ordered. Jesus, he'd been really out of it.

Derick and Siobhan looked across the table at each other, and Derick wondered how he'd let a table come between them. As the silence stretched out, both of them started raising their eyebrows at the other, creating a standoff about who should start the discussion. Finally, the two of them started laughing.

"I guess we should talk?"

The server dropped off waters, and Siobhan took a long drink. "About what?" she asked.

"About us?" This time it really was a question.

Siobhan folded her hands on top of the table. "Haven't we already done a lot of that?"

Derick let out a soft chuckle. "Yeah, we have."

"I'm not sure anything else needs to be said. We've both shared how we felt ad nauseam. And you showing up today says everything about where we're going from here. I think we're good."

Derick leaned toward her. "Then what are we doing here?"

"I have no idea."

Derick nodded, called his driver, and signaled for the server. When she arrived, Derick handed her a twenty before ushering Siobhan toward the exit and into his SUV.

The ride back to his apartment was filled with roving hands and passionate kisses. The urgency of the night almost a month ago was gone, but the anticipation was stronger than ever.

Once in his apartment, they wasted no time. They tore the clothes from each other, dropping them along the path toward Derick's bedroom. A few times, they laughed at their savage desire. There was a lightness to their lust. Derick felt like he was burning to the ground and levitating into the air. It was something he'd only ever felt with Siobhan and something he'd never take for granted.

Derick lifted Siobhan, who immediately wrapped her legs around his waist, then walked into his room and dropped her on the bed, causing her to bounce slightly. They smiled at each other before their gazes locked, and the amusement was replaced by yearning. He lowered himself on top of her and claimed her mouth.

Her tongue eagerly met his, but she let him lead the kiss, which he was thankful for. Derick needed to run this show. He needed to pour every ounce of what she meant to him into this experience. Needed her to know that she was his.

His mouth kissed along her jaw, moving toward her ear. He sucked on the lobe before whispering, "You are never leaving me again."

"No. Never."

"It wasn't a question," he growled. He slid his cock against her clit, causing her to moan.

"Please, Derick."

He brought a hand up to her neck and caressed the skin there. "Please what?" He placed kisses on the soft skin below his hand. "Tell me what you need, and then trust me to give it to you."

She groaned as he ground his achingly hard cock against her. His mouth moved down to suck on one of her nipples, which caused her to arch off the bed. "Make love to me," she whispered.

"Always," he replied as he moved to the other nipple.

"But not soft."

His tongue continued to tease the sensitive bud. "How do you want it?"

She pushed her hands into his hair, keeping his mouth on her.

"Answer me, Siobhan."

She moaned again. "Hard. I need…I can't…just…"

Derick moved back up so that he could look her in the eyes. He saw the tears swimming there. He moved his fingers so that he could lightly comb them through her hair. "I know, baby. Me, too."

And he did know. They needed to forge a new bond, and this one needed to be unbreakable. She needed them to be one in every way possible. He did, too. They were incomplete alone. Erasing that feeling of desperate loneliness wasn't enough. It needed to be shattered. "Trust me?" he asked.

"Yes." The look in her eyes spoke to the truth of her words.

He smiled at her. "Then reach up and grab the headboard."

Her face relaxed and she instantly complied.

He sat back on his heels between her spread legs and looked at her. His fingers traced over her skin, leaving a trail of goose bumps in their wake.

Siobhan writhed beneath him, but she didn't take her hands away from the headboard and she didn't attempt to regain some control by pushing up into his hands. She was pliant and submissive beneath him.

Which made his cock impossibly harder. Unable to hold back, he let his fingers wander to the apex of her thighs. He rubbed circles over her clit as the fingers of his other hand pushed deep inside of her.

"Oh, my God," she moaned. Her hips swayed into his movements, her body close to quaking.

"I can't wait to put my cock inside of you."

"Don't…don't wait. I need it."

He withdrew his hand and used her wetness to slick himself. Then he moved his body above her again. "Look at me."

Siobhan opened her eyes, and the desire and adoration he saw there almost made him lose it.

"I love you," he said as he pushed his cock to the hilt inside of her.

Her hands gripped the headboard as she locked her elbows so his thrusts wouldn't move her up the bed. "I love you, too," she said. "So much."

His next thrust made speaking impossible for either of them. He rocked his hips into her, his sac slapping against her ass. Their moans and groans were guttural, the sound of his cock sliding in and out of her obscene. He continued to pump into her, chasing both of their orgasms.

Her pants became more erratic, her body wound tighter. She threw her head back as she convulsed. The throbbing pulse of her release made his balls tighten as a tingle raced up his spine.

Derick dropped to his elbows as he caged her body in. He pumped his hips furiously. Closing his eyes tightly, he shuddered as he came.

Spent, he collapsed into her, and buried his face in her hair. Their sweat-slicked bodies began to shiver as the heat they had created began to dissipate. But neither of them made any attempt to move.

Derick felt Siobhan's fingernails scrape lightly along his back. He lifted his head to look at her. "Hey," he whispered before pressing a soft kiss to her lips. He felt her smile.

"Hey."

Resting his forehead on top of hers, he basked in the closeness that he once foolishly thought he could live without.

Siobhan's hands began to roam again, and Derick couldn't resist rocking against her as his cock began to perk back up.

She gasped. "You want me again?"

"I'll always want you," he replied. He kissed her deeply, and then trailed his lips down her neck. "I also have to teach you a lesson."

"For what?" she asked on a laugh that sounded more like a sigh.

He lifted his head so his eyes could connect with hers. "Did I tell you to let go of the headboard?"

Siobhan's eyes widened. Then her mouth twisted into a delicious grin. She took her hands off of him and made a show of pushing them up the bed so she could grip the headboard.

"That's more like it," he said. And he made sure she more than liked everything that followed.

Chapter 26

SIOBHAN ROLLED OVER and snuggled into Derick.

"Don't even try it. You've rendered me completely useless," Derick said, teasing clear in his tone.

Siobhan shifted up onto an elbow so she could look at him. "Who? Me?" she asked innocently. She drifted her fingertips over his chest lightly.

He caught her hand in his and pressed it flat against his skin. "Stop it."

"What am I doing?"

"Making me hard."

She leaned down to press kisses to his shoulder. "I thought you said you were useless."

"I am. I think it would take divine intervention for me to get off again."

She narrowed her eyes at him. "That sounds like a challenge."

Derick burst out laughing. "It definitely wasn't meant that way."

"But what if I took it that way? What if I climbed on top of you and rode you? You think you could come then?"

Derick's eyes were locked on hers, desire clear on his face. "Maybe you should try and find out."

Siobhan smiled as she leaned to press a kiss to his lips. She flung a leg over him so that she was straddling his thighs, her breasts pushed against his torso. Rocking slightly, she let her nipples be stimulated by his chest hair and firm body. Eventually, she leaned forward a little and then sat back, taking his cock all the way inside of her. She straightened up and began to move up and down on him.

"Jesus Christ," he muttered as his hands moved to her hips, gripping tightly.

"You've really found religion in this bedroom today," she teased, despite barely having the breath to utter the words.

"I found something. God, that's so good."

Siobhan couldn't help but smirk at his response. But her lips quickly parted as Derick began to thrust up into her.

She moved a hand up her body to toy with her nipple. Since she'd already had three orgasms in as many hours, Siobhan's nerve endings were overly sensitive. It wasn't going to take her long to reach her climax.

"Touch your clit, Siobhan. I wanna watch you get yourself off while you ride me."

She pinched her nipple one last time before sliding her hand down her body. When her fingertips made contact with her clit, she jolted at the sensation.

"You're close, aren't you?"

Derick's words weren't helping her refrain from orgasming.

She felt like she was one dirty word away from losing control. So she decided to fight fire with fire. "I want you to come inside me, Derick."

He gritted his teeth and thrust harder, but didn't reply.

"Come on. Fill me up. I want it. Wanna feel you dripping out of me for the rest of the night."

Derick's grip tightened and he pistoned into her.

She ground into him, letting his cock go even deeper. Then she bounced up and down on him a few more times before she felt his body go rigid and slickness fill her. She'd been giving her clit lazy strokes, but Derick's release made her pick up the pace.

His hands reached up and caressed her breasts before he began rolling her nipples between his fingers.

It was all she needed. She shuddered on top of him as she rode out the waves of pleasure. The orgasm was powerful but brief as exhaustion won out. She collapsed on his chest.

"You okay there, champ?" Derick asked, with obvious amusement.

"You came again. I win," she mumbled against his chest.

"I'm pretty sure we both won."

"Very true. But now *I'm* broken. And I need to go into work tonight."

Derick tightened his arms around her. "That's not going to work for me."

Siobhan chuckled and then propped her head on her hands so she could see him. "What? Were you planning on keeping me here forever as your sex slave?"

"Don't be ridiculous," he scoffed. "It couldn't be forever."

She slapped his shoulder lightly and he laughed.

But his face grew serious quickly. "You really have to go?"

She sighed. "Unfortunately. But I don't work tomorrow. We could do something then?"

"All right. I guess I can make it without you until then."

"Sorry for your suffering," she said as she kissed him. Then she pushed off of him and began to grab her clothes.

"You need to leave right *now?*" he asked.

"Well…yeah. I need to go home and change my clothes. It'll be easier for me to shower there."

Derick simply nodded, and then got out of bed and began dressing, too.

"You don't need to get dressed just to walk me to the elevator," she joked.

"I'm not walking you to the elevator."

She looked at him, confusion probably plain on her face. "Then what are you doing?"

"Going home with you."

"Why? Not that I don't love your company," she added quickly. "But…why?"

Derick walked over to her and wrapped his arms around her. "Because I'm not ready for today to be over." He kissed her deeply then, emotion pouring from both of them.

"Okay then," she said when they broke apart. "You can meet my roommate, Dom." Siobhan walked out of the bedroom to collect the rest of her clothes, and Derick followed.

"Cool. Is he a nice guy?"

"Yeah."

"What's his story?"

Siobhan threw a smile over her shoulder. "I actually have no idea."

Derick huffed. "Sounds like you guys have really bonded."

Siobhan laughed at Derick's dry delivery. She suddenly realized that she'd laughed more in the past four hours than she'd laughed in the entire time she'd been without Derick. There was no longer any denying it: Derick made her life better. It was time she started returning the favor.

Chapter 27

DERICK RAISED THE glass to his nostrils and breathed in the aroma. No matter how many times he'd tasted fine wine, he never got any better at evaluating it. Especially before he even tried it. The scents could range from nail polish remover to plums, and that didn't necessarily indicate what it would taste like once it entered his mouth.

This one smelled like cardboard, and Derick felt his nose turn up reflexively as he inhaled.

"Something wrong, sir?" the waiter asked.

"I'm not sure about this one." He smelled it again and then raised his eyes toward Siobhan, who was seated across from him looking slightly amused.

She held out her hand. "May I?" she asked.

"By all means," Derick said, passing the glass to her as the waiter stood patiently beside the table.

She swirled the glass in the air for several moments and then brought it to her nose, closing her eyes as she inhaled. Then she took a sip.

Derick could see her moving the wine around in her mouth before swallowing it. She set the glass down and nodded toward the waiter, indicating she approved.

"Looks like we'll take that one after all," Derick said.

The waiter gave him a quick nod and poured them each a glass before setting the bottle on the table. Then he told them the specials for the night, and said he would return to take their orders shortly.

As soon as he was out of earshot, Derick inched toward Siobhan, his hands clasped in front of him on the table. "That was impressive," he said with a raised eyebrow. "Not to mention sexy as hell."

"What was?" she asked, glancing up from her menu.

"Tasting the wine. I still have to swirl it flat on the table or it splashes out of the glass."

Siobhan laughed softly.

"I'm glad I know you can do it because it's your job from now on. I'm no good at it, and watching you move it around in your mouth before you swallow is an added bonus."

Her eyes twinkled with amusement. Derick could tell she was trying to suppress a smile when she spoke. "You really have a knack for making the strangest things seem dirty."

"Thanks," he said, grinning widely and sitting up a little straighter. "Do you know what you're getting?" he asked, finally bringing his attention away from Siobhan and toward his menu.

"I don't know. The pecan-encrusted trout special sounded pretty good. I might go with that."

Derick nodded as he eyed up the steak choices. "Trout's too…fishy for me."

"Well, it's a fish, so…" she trailed off.

"Yeah, but some fish don't really taste like fish. Flounder and tilapia are soft and light, and salmon and mahimahi have more of a chicken texture and the seasonings tend to disguise any fish flavor that they—" Derick stopped midthought when he noticed Siobhan's eyes getting wider. "What?" he asked.

She shrugged. "Nothing. I just didn't realize you were such a seafood connoisseur, that's all."

Derick chuckled and closed his menu. "What can I say? I'm a man of many talents."

Siobhan's eyes locked on his and her lips parted slightly so she could press her teeth against her bottom one. "Well, I definitely can't argue with that," she replied.

The waiter came back to take their orders and pour them another glass of wine. Full of easy conversation, the dinner passed quickly. They discussed everything from the movie they'd seen the other night to the new app Derick was helping to develop that allowed people to upload pictures of bugs and animals in order to identify them.

"That's a good idea. I could've used that the other day. I found some shiny silver thing in the shower."

Derick stared at her as he tried to keep from smirking. "The faucet?"

"No, you ass. It was a bug. And it was slimy."

Derick's eyes widened. "You touched it?"

Siobhan looked disgusted. "No," she said, shaking her head. "I didn't…it just *looked* like it would've been slimy."

Derick nodded as he swallowed his bite of mashed potatoes. "Okay. I have a serious question," he said when he was done.

Siobhan looked slightly nervous. "What is it?"

Derick stared at her, letting the seriousness of his expression sink in. "Who do you think you know better? The bug or your roommate?"

Siobhan rolled her eyes and laughed. "Shut up," she joked. "I told you Dom was Blaine's friend from high school. That's all I really need to know. I only care that he's not a serial killer. I don't need to know his favorite color. Besides," she added, "the gallery's actually starting to make some money. Every artist has sold at least a few pieces, including me. Hopefully I should be able to get a place of my own soon."

He resisted the urge to ask her if she really wanted to live by herself. Though the past few weeks had been easy and comfortable between them, Derick knew it was too soon to discuss living together.

The thought made him smile, but he didn't want to bring up that discussion now. Not when Siobhan seemed so confident and relaxed, like all the pieces were starting to fall into place. She even mentioned the possibility of quitting the Stone Room and making art and the gallery her sole career—a dream she'd never thought she'd be able to accomplish.

It made Derick happy in a way that nothing else in his life ever had. His eyes crinkled, lighting up with his excitement for her.

"What?" she asked. "Why do you have the goofy grin on your face?"

Derick realized he'd probably been staring at her for too long without contributing to the conversation. "No reason. Just happy," he said, reaching a hand across the table to clasp hers.

She brought his hand up to her lips and gave it a gentle kiss before speaking against it. "I'm happy, too," she said softly.

And Derick knew it was the truth.

Chapter 28

SIOBHAN ENTERED THE back of the gallery with Derick following behind her. "So what are we doing here?" he asked.

She flashed him a mischievous grin over her shoulder. "It's a surprise," she answered as she flipped on the lights.

Derick's eyes flitted from painting to painting. He hadn't been in the gallery since the opening just over a month ago. That night, he'd been so preoccupied with the artwork Siobhan had painted that he hadn't even gotten the chance to look at the other artists' pieces.

He was wandering over toward some abstract-looking cityscapes when he heard Siobhan's voice.

"You gonna stand around all night or you gonna give me a hand?"

Derick turned around to see her smiling, a large roll of brown paper under her arm. "Of course," he said, moving toward her. "What do you need help with?"

"Some of these paintings need to get wrapped up so they can get shipped. I'll print the address labels if you can get the paintings down and start wrapping them. There's bubble wrap in the back," she said. "I'll go grab that and some packaging tape."

"Which ones have to come down?" Derick asked once she'd returned with the other supplies.

She looked at a paper on the desk. "The first two portraits on that wall, that one with the bright red over there, and…" She scanned the paper. "And mine, but they're already in the back room."

"How many did you sell?" he asked.

"All of them." When she looked up at him, Derick's smile was even brighter than hers.

He closed the remaining distance between them and wrapped his arms around her, sweeping her up into an embrace. "Seriously? You sold everything?"

She nodded. "Mm-hmm." She looked over at her paintings. "I sold a few during opening night, and then someone else came in the other night and bought the rest. I wasn't even here when it happened."

Derick put her down and held her head as he kissed her excitedly. "That's incredible!"

Siobhan breathed in deeply before letting out what sounded like a sigh of relief. "It really is." Then she lifted an eyebrow at him. "You've never gone by the name Wyatt, have you?"

"No, definitely not," Derick said quickly, an awkward smile gracing his lips. "I promise I didn't buy them this time."

She laughed. "I'm just messing with you," she said.

"I *am* actually a little sad that you sold the ones you painted about us, though. I would've loved to have had them." He pulled back to look her in the eyes. "With your permission, of course."

Siobhan looked over her shoulder at the wall of paintings. "You can't buy them, Derick," she said when she turned back to him.

"I understand. I didn't mean—"

"No, you don't understand. You can't buy them because they were never for sale." She smiled faintly, her eyes softening with emotion. "The ones I sold were other ones I posted on the gallery website when a few buyers asked to see more of my work. They wanted these," she said, pointing to the ones on the wall. "But I refused to sell them. They're yours, Derick. I painted them for *you*."

Silent for a moment, he didn't do anything except wrap his arms tightly around her, feeling her heartbeat against him. "Thank you," he said simply, as the magnitude of her actions hit him. The only paintings she'd displayed on her opening night were ones she didn't have any intention of selling. And it had all been to show her devotion to him. Derick eyed the paintings again. "What do you think I should do with them?"

"Typically people hang them."

Derick reached down to squeeze her right above her hips, making her squeal. "I meant *where* should I hang them?"

Siobhan shrugged. "That's up to you. They're yours, remember?"

Derick smiled, tucking her soft hair behind her ear. *"Ours,"* he corrected her. When she didn't argue, he planted a gentle kiss on her forehead before releasing her and walking over toward the artwork on the wall. He removed a few of the paintings and set them down carefully. "We should celebrate," he said.

Siobhan cut some brown paper from the roll and looked up at him as he took down the last of the paintings. "We should," she said. "What'd you have in mind?"

Chapter 29

WE SHOULD CELEBRATE all the time," Siobhan said softly as Derick nibbled on the sensitive skin right below her ear. They'd been back at Derick's apartment for only about twenty minutes, but hadn't wasted any time in getting lost in each other.

Derick let out a chuckle. "Why?" Derick had stopped kissing her to respond, which made her regret talking in the first place.

"Because apparently I'm a fan of expensive champagne and your mouth, so if this is what happens when I get good news, I'm not above making something up." She laughed, which was probably more due to the fact that she was on her fourth drink than because she'd said something funny. "What is this anyway?" she asked, as she took the last sip of what was left in her flute. "I don't usually like champagne."

Derick smiled against her collarbone as he removed the glass from her hand and set it on the table next to his couch. "Less talking, more nudity," he said, pulling her shirt over her head with a sudden urgency.

Siobhan felt it, too—the heat growing between them, their heartbeats quickening as they tore off layers of clothing.

Their breaths were already heavy with the need for each other, and Siobhan could feel how hot her skin was from alcohol and desire. This was where she belonged. In Derick Miller's arms as he ran his hands all over her body and made love to her mouth with his tongue.

God, that tongue. It was so soft, but so aggressive and consuming that she nearly forgot to breathe. And when she finally did, she found herself gasping for air.

She'd been so preoccupied with his wet lips on her, Siobhan hadn't even realized that Derick had leaned her back onto the couch so he could lie on top of her.

But once she noticed Derick's weight on top of her, it was all she could think about. Well, that and his erection pressing against her in just the right place. Her legs wrapped instinctively around him, but he didn't push inside her, choosing instead to inflict delicious torture as he slipped his cock over her clit, pressing his tip lightly against her until her body was pleading with him to go all the way inside.

"I'm not above begging, Derick. Please. God, please. You're gonna make me come like this," she said as he pulled at her nipple.

"Not yet," he rasped, his facial hair brushing against her smooth skin. "Together."

Siobhan released the air she'd been holding in a huff as she tried to calm her stimulated nerve endings and focus on anything other than the beautiful man on top of her whose solid biceps she was currently gripping as he ground against her. "You seriously need to stop then."

He looked down at her, amusement in his eyes as he slowed his movements to a speed that had her teetering on the edge without falling over it. "Not stopping," he said.

Gradually, his expression became more serious, his eyes closing as she guessed he was trying to hold back, too.

"Please. Derick, I want…"

"What do you want?" he asked, his motion ceasing completely as he looked down at her.

She returned his gaze, a fire burning in their eyes that was impossible to extinguish. "You. I want you."

Derick was still for a moment as his expression softened. Then he stood, his cock thick and heavy as he walked to the end of the couch, grabbed Siobhan's ankles and yanked her toward him until her ass was on the armrest of the couch and her legs hung over the edge.

He grabbed her thighs, spreading them wide so he could fit between them. Siobhan's head was already fuzzy from the position, and when Derick finally thrust inside her, she thought she might pass out from the pleasure.

Her body immediately conformed to accommodate his as she submitted to him, arching her back off the leather cushion as he gripped her hips and held her up so he could plunge deep inside her.

The pressure built inside her until she knew she'd explode any moment. "Harder. God, harder," she said, though she wasn't sure if he could even comply with her request. He was already driving into her with such force, she was inching back with every thrust.

She knew they were both so close to losing control as she felt each of their bodies tense with the hope of prolonging the pleasure. Derick's shaky groan was what did her in, and the orgasm she'd been fighting came with a force she hadn't felt before.

Maybe it was the blood rushing to her head, or the alcohol, or that she was at Derick's mercy. Or maybe it was because this man did things to her that could never be explained. Whatever it was, it had her quaking beneath him as his cock jerked inside her and filled her with his warm release.

When the aftershocks of their orgasms had finally faded enough to allow them to break contact, Derick pulled out of her, his erection still firm though somewhat weaker. She thought about asking him if he had round two in him, but since she couldn't even find the strength to ask, she figured she was too spent to follow through even if he could.

"You've exhausted me," she said.

With a satisfied smile on his face, Derick extended his hands so he could help her up. "I think I know something that'll relax you."

Chapter 30

TOSSING HER BAG on her bed, Siobhan headed for the bathroom to get ready for work. She had about twenty-five minutes before she had to leave for her shift at the Stone Room. She'd spent most of the day at the gallery. Now that it was fully up and running, she was on her own to do most of the work herself.

Not that she minded. It was the most rewarding job she'd ever had. The artists were grateful to have their work shown, and they'd all been selling paintings steadily over the past few months. The phrase "beginner's luck" popped into her mind, but she quickly pushed it out.

The gallery would succeed. *She* would succeed. She had to. She had too much to pay forward to fail.

She pulled a brush through her hair and reapplied her makeup—darker eye shadow and a lipstick that was a shade of red she'd never think to wear during the day. Then she put on a little bronzer to bring some life into her complexion. It was only the beginning of spring, and her skin still lacked the color she'd like it to have.

When she got back to her room, she took off the clothes she'd worn all day and was heading to her small closet to choose the black outfit she'd wear for the night when there was a knock at her bedroom door.

"Hold on. I'm not wearing anything," she said. She definitely didn't want Dom seeing her in only her bra and underwear.

Siobhan heard the door open anyway and she quickly ran to the bed on the other side of the room to grab a blanket to cover up. "What the hell are—"

"I thought you said you were naked?"

She knew that voice. And it wasn't Dom's. "Derick?" she said as she turned around. "What are you doing?"

"Well, I *thought* I was gonna get to see you without clothes on, but now I'm disappointed," he said, a sly grin crinkling his eyes.

"I thought you were Dom." She dropped the blanket back on the bed with a relieved sigh and shook her head. "And what are you doing *here?*" she asked.

"I came to give you a ride. I figured you could use a break from the subway."

"Oh. Um, okay. Thanks. That's sweet," she said, returning to her closet after giving him a quick kiss. "I'm almost ready. I just need to put something on."

"I disagree," Derick said, putting a finger to his lips. "I feel like less is more."

She raised an eyebrow at him. "You really want me escorting wealthy businessmen to tables in only a bra and underwear?"

He thought for a moment. "You do have a point. But I'm not taking you to work."

Her eyes narrowed, prompting Derick to explain, but he didn't. "I thought you said you were giving me a ride?"

"I know."

"So...?"

"So I'm giving you a ride, but not to the Stone Room," he said, an amused grin spreading across his face. He put a hand into the pocket of his fitted gray pants and threw a nod toward her bedroom door. "Come on," he said. "Better get dressed or we're gonna be late." Then he laughed in a way that made Siobhan want to kiss him and throw something at him at the same time.

"I know I'm going to be late. To *work*. I can't go somewhere else right now."

Derick shrugged. "Sure you can."

She opened her mouth to protest, but Derick reached out and put a finger under her chin to close it. "I thought you said you trusted me?"

His tone didn't match the seriousness of his words, and his expression told her this game was amusing him more than she'd like it to.

She breathed in deeply and let out an exaggerated exhale. "I do," she said.

"Good." He walked to her closet and stared for a few seconds before handing her a fitted, royal-blue, long-sleeve dress that was probably too short for the early April weather. "Wear this. It brings out your eyes," he said. "And you look hot in it."

Trying to suppress a smile, Siobhan felt her insides nearly melt at his words. Then she reached out and grabbed the hanger from his hand. "The blue dress it is."

Chapter 31

SIOBHAN WAS NEARLY bouncing next to him in the SUV. She was excited, but the responsible part of her was a bit worried about her job. "Saul knows I'm not coming in tonight, right?"

"Yes," he said, placing a hand on her thigh. The gesture was an innocent one, but even that small bit of contact had her hoping he would move his hand higher. "He knows you won't be there."

"And he's okay with it? Because after that stunt I pulled the night I left to go home with you, I'm pretty sure his tolerance for my bullshit is lower than it's ever been."

Derick rolled his eyes playfully. "Yes, he's okay with it. Now would you try to relax? We have a long flight ahead of us."

His eyes darted quickly to the window and away from hers, which she could feel widening. "Flight? Where are we going? For how long? I didn't even pack a bag. Who's taking care of the gallery?"

Derick's gaze remained fixed on the outside world as they drove, his lips pressed into a small grin.

She grabbed his arm and tried to pull him toward her, but the effort was futile. It was like trying to move a truck. "Hey," she said, now unbuckling her seat belt so she could climb onto him. "Would you care to elaborate a little or do you plan to ignore my question?"

"I'm still deciding," he replied with a smirk.

She was straddling him now, and she gripped his hands to pin them on either side of his head. "Tell me," she demanded, though her voice came out more like a plea.

Derick laughed. "You do realize I *let* you put my hands here, right? I could easily get out of it."

"Tell me," she said again, this time raising herself off of him so she could plop back down onto his lap.

Derick let out a grunt at the contact. Then he removed his hands from where Siobhan had put them and grabbed her hips so he could lift her off of him and put her back in her seat. "Fine. But put your seat belt back on. It's dangerous for you to be on top of me like that."

Siobhan raised her eyebrows at the unintended meaning of his words, but she complied.

When the seat belt clicked into place he spoke. "I had Blaine pack you a bag, and I contacted Liza. Since she was interim curator, she's capable of handling things while you're away. But since this is the actual celebration for the success of the gallery, where we're going and for how long stays a surprise for now," he said.

Siobhan inhaled deeply and let out a sigh that was equal parts frustration and appreciation. "Fine," she said.

Derick gave her a firm nod. "Good."

The rest of the drive to the airport was filled mostly with playfully seductive glances. Siobhan found herself wanting to get to wherever it was they were going, if for no other reason than to get back on top of Derick. Though it would definitely be sans clothes the next time.

By the time they arrived on the tarmac, Siobhan nearly jumped out of the SUV when the driver opened the door. She looked at the jet nearby and wondered if that was Derick's. It was bigger than she'd imagined, but she didn't see another one close to them that it could possibly be. "Is that seriously yours?" she asked.

He nodded as the driver opened the trunk and removed two bags. "Yup."

"It's huge."

Clearly amused, Derick laughed. "That's what she said."

Siobhan punched him in the arm, though she couldn't help but laugh. "You're so immature sometimes," she said. "I kind of love it, though."

He smiled and extended an arm toward the steps of the plane. "After you," he said.

She climbed the steps and entered the plane, where they were immediately greeted by the pilot. Siobhan's eyes widened as she took in her surroundings. The white leather seats were roomier than any she'd ever sat on when she'd flown commercial. And the windows were significantly larger as well.

She sat down in a seat and gazed out the window at the darkening sky as she waited for Derick to stop talking to the pilot. A minute or so later, he walked toward her. "What are you doing?"

Confused by the question, Siobhan looked around her. "Uh, sitting," she said slowly.

"I see that," Derick said. "But this section's for the crew. Our area is back there." He held out his hand to help her up.

He has a crew? These seats were nicer than first class—or what she'd seen of it on her way back to coach—and this wasn't even where they would be sitting during the flight.

When Siobhan stood, Derick leaned in and whispered in her ear, "Come on. Let me show you how big my jet is."

She bit back a laugh as Derick led her into the main area of the aircraft. She could easily forget she was on a plane if not for the circular windows that ran the length of the living area. In addition to the luxury seating, there was a full sofa across from a flat-screen TV that was anchored to the wall and a conference table with large leather seats surrounding it.

She put her purse down on one of the nearby seats and ran her hand along the sleek wooden table. "This is incredible," she said.

Derick smiled as a man and woman walked into their quarters.

The crew, she thought with a smile.

"Siobhan," Derick said. "This is Katherine and Richard."

Siobhan extended her hand to greet the two.

"It's a pleasure to finally meet you, Miss Dempsey," Katherine said. "Please let us know if there is anything we can get for you during the flight."

"Yes," Richard said. "We'll be serving dinner shortly. Please help yourself to the hors d'oeuvres." He gestured behind him to the table with food and plates. "What can I offer you to drink?" he asked.

Chapter 32

DERICK."

He heard the warning in her voice. Maybe the time for playing games was over. "Technically Rafael is taking us."

"What? Who's that?"

"The pilot you just met." He couldn't help laughing. She was so cute when she was flustered.

"Oh, yeah. I knew that." She looked around the plane once more before settling her gaze back on him. "Really? Italy?"

And here it was: make or break time. Either she was telling the whole truth when she'd said she accepted him for who he was, or she wasn't. "Yes, really. You once told me that every aspiring artist should go there, but I missed out on taking you when that label still applied to you. Now that you're an *established* artist..." he shrugged. "I thought it was time."

She bit the corner of her bottom lip and he could practically see her thinking. After a few moments, her body seemed to relax. "Blaine better have packed the right clothes or I'll never speak to her again."

She couldn't place his accent, which sounded a bit like an Australian one. *New Zealand, maybe?* "Water would be great for now. Thank you."

Richard looked toward Derick, who asked for an unsweetened iced tea and a bottle of some kind of wine even the Stone Room didn't serve.

When Richard left, Siobhan headed over to the spread of food that had been put out just for them. Though she was hungry, there was no way they'd possibly eat even half of this, and it was only the first course. She looked at the calamari, bruschetta, antipasto, and various types of fresh bread, unsure where to start.

When she looked up at Derick, he shrugged. "I remembered that you told me you love all things Italian on our first official date."

"Well, yeah, who doesn't like Italian? I mean…" Siobhan's words trailed off as things began to click in her brain. Once the full picture came together, she stared at her sneaky boyfriend. "Derick. Don't tell me you're taking me to Italy."

Derick's lips twitched as though he was trying to fight a smile. "Okay. I won't tell you."

Derick felt his own body relax. He took two large steps and swept her into an embrace. "So this is okay?"

She gave his waist a squeeze. "It's more than okay. I'm not sure I deserve how good you are to me, but I'm thankful for it all the same."

He held on to her for a bit longer, before he forced himself to pull back. "We should sit down so we can take off."

Smiling at him, she lifted up on her tiptoes and pressed a kiss to his cheek. "Sounds good."

Once in the air, the crew served them dinner, and Derick shared the tentative itinerary he'd mapped out. "We'll land in Pisa, and a car will be waiting to drive us to Florence. I figured we could see the Leaning Tower of Pisa on our way out of the city since it's kind of a tourist must. We should arrive by late afternoon."

Siobhan bounced in her seat. "I'm so excited."

"Good. Then let's let Katherine and Richard clean up dinner so we can relax."

Siobhan stood, but hesitated, looked at Derick, then back at her empty plate.

"What's wrong?" he asked.

"It feels weird to make them clean up after us."

"Weirder than trying to find out where things belong on a jet you've never been on before?" Derick teased. "You clean up after people all the time at work. Let someone do it for you for once." He made his way to one of the seats by a window.

Siobhan followed, her eyes glued out the window. "I love watching the view from up here."

"Me, too," Derick replied. But he wasn't staring out a window. His eyes were locked on Siobhan. A fact she realized when she turned to look at him.

"Is there a bed on this plane?" she asked.

Derick snorted a laugh. "What do you think?"

"I think you'd better show it to me."

Derick unbuckled both of their seat belts and stood, holding a hand out to Siobhan, which she promptly took. He led her to a wooden pocket door that he pushed open and motioned for her to enter. He followed, closing and locking the door behind him.

She turned instantly, their bodies fitting together perfectly as her hands slid up his chest and around his neck while his wound around her waist and settled on her ass, pulling her into him.

Pressing his erection into her, he could barely contain a groan of pleasure. He nipped along her jaw as her hands tangled in his hair. Needing her naked, he reached down and pulled her dress over her head. Their mouths quickly found each other again as their hands moved in tandem to take his clothes off.

Siobhan reached behind her back to unclasp her bra. She moved her hands to her thong, but Derick stopped them.

"Let me," he said. He sank to his knees and pulled her lace thong down her body slowly, pressing light kisses to her thighs on the way. Once he had them down, she lifted a leg so he could slip them over her black high heels. "Leave the shoes on."

Siobhan moaned her response.

Derick kissed his way back up her legs to her apex. Dragging his hands up the inside of her thighs to her slick folds, he parted them before leaning in to flick his tongue against her clit.

Her hands instantly threaded through his hair as she arched her back and moaned again.

He continued to lavish his attention on her, stimulating her sensitive nub with his tongue as his finger found its way inside of her.

"Oh, my God."

"Like that?" he asked.

"Don't ask stupid questions right now," she replied between panting breaths.

He chuckled before returning to the task before him. There were so many things he found arousing about Siobhan, but there was a special eroticism to tasting her like this, feeling her coming undone on his tongue. His cock was hard and heavy, but he didn't dare take his hands off of Siobhan to touch himself. He could wait.

"Derick. I'm going to come." Her fingers tightened in his hair, and she bent forward slightly as if her body were bracing for the orgasm that was about to overpower it. Seconds later, she groaned loudly as her entire body convulsed. Her clit throbbed under his tongue as her walls constricted around his fingers.

Derick kept up his assault until he felt the last of her release work its way through her body. Then he quickly stood, hoisting her up on the way, and carried her to the bed. He kneeled on the bed, lowering them both down together. Unable to waste a single additional second, he pushed into her with one hard thrust.

Her fingernails scored down his back as he rocked into her. The slickness between her thighs made his movements in and out of her smoother, allowed him to go deeper.

Need burned through him. The entire evening was all too much: He'd been able to surprise her, and she'd easily accepted his gift. And God, did she look amazing. Derick couldn't quell the feelings inside him; there was no slowing down and making it last. And as he felt his skin begin to tingle, he pumped faster, chasing the wave of pleasure that was so intense he worried he'd drown in the feeling.

Seconds later he was coming. And his physical release was emotional as well. He let go of every doubt and worry and regret. Uncoiled, he basked in the glow of knowing he was exactly where he was supposed to be with exactly who he was meant to be there with.

He continued to push softly into her, his cock still hard inside of her. He reached down to stroke her clit, bringing her to orgasm again. And as he watched her fall apart beneath him, he knew that Italy would mark a new beginning for them both.

Chapter 33

I SERIOUSLY CANNOT believe we're here," Siobhan said as she placed a hand on her chest. "I'm standing in front of *The Birth of Venus* right now." She turned to look at Derick. "Botticelli painted that," she continued as she motioned to the painting. "And I'm standing here looking at it."

Derick smiled. She'd had a similar reaction to almost every painting she'd seen since they'd entered the Uffizi Gallery in central Florence.

They'd elected to stay in and order dinner to their room when they'd arrived the previous day, but Siobhan had been adamant about getting up early to see the sights. So after having a nice breakfast on the terrace of their private Garden Suite at the Four Seasons in Florence, they'd called for a car and been on their way.

Derick loved watching her take in all of the famous art around her. She approached each piece with a reverence that made him wish he knew more about the art on the walls. Other than the famous names—Rembrandt, Da Vinci, Michelangelo—Derick really didn't know what he was looking at.

So he settled for looking at Siobhan instead.

She wandered around the gallery for over three hours, looking at some things multiple times as if she were trying to commit every detail to memory.

It allowed Derick to commit every detail about *her* to memory. The way her breath quickened when she was excited. The way her eyes lit up when she noticed something new. How she'd fiddle with the ends of her hair as she examined the canvases as if each brushstroke had a story to tell.

They exited the museum hand in hand and started toward the building adjacent to the Uffizi Gallery, the Loggia dei Lanzi. They walked under the large arches that opened onto the street and began surveying the sculptures inside. Derick knew even less about what he was seeing there than he had at the museum, but he could tell that most of the sculptures depicted heroes and gods from Roman mythology.

Once they'd seen everything there was to see, they made their way across the square, past the replica of Michelangelo's *David,* and into a café for a late lunch. After they'd ordered, Siobhan settled back into her chair. "There's so much to see. It's almost overwhelming."

"Hey, this is a fun, no-stress trip," he teased. "We have five more days in Florence. And we can always come back if there's stuff we miss."

Her gaze, which had been taking in the square outside the café, flew to his. Then her mouth broke into a wide smile. "Yeah. I guess we can."

Chapter 34

THREE DAYS INTO their trip, Siobhan and Derick strolled hand in hand through the Piazza della Repubblica. Despite the early hour, the square was filled with people. Some were shopping at the stores, others were eating at the surrounding restaurants.

Siobhan stopped to watch some street performers, two mimes who had drawn a small crowd of onlookers. "I've never seen a mime before," she said, in awe of how he could silently express real emotion. His eyes spoke in a way that Siobhan couldn't manage with words. It was an entirely different form of art than what she was familiar with.

"I don't think I have, either," Derick said. "At least not that I remember."

The mimes finished their performance, and Derick tossed some money into the bucket on the ground before they turned away.

"The only thing that bothers me is that mimes always seem so sad," Siobhan said, turning to look up at Derick as they walked across the square.

"I don't think they're *always* sad." He laughed a bit before speaking again. "Just...most of the time."

Siobhan laughed, too, and swung Derick's hand as she held it. It made her feel lighter, more carefree than she had a moment ago watching the performance. "I know what we should do," she said suddenly.

"What?"

Siobhan pointed across the square, and Derick's happy expression transformed into one of clear hesitation when he saw the carousel. "No way. I'm a grown man. I can't go on a merry-go-round."

"There are adults on there."

"They have their children with them. I have you," he said with a laugh.

She let go of his hand and shoved him playfully. "Come on. It'll be fun. I haven't been on one since I was a kid."

"There's a reason for that." Derick rolled his eyes and kept his feet firmly planted on the ground, but Siobhan knew that wouldn't last long.

"Well, *I'm* going on," she said simply. She started heading toward the ride again when she heard his voice behind her.

"You can't go on by yourself," Derick called. "That'll look even stranger."

They approached the antique carousel, which they quickly learned was from the early 1900s and belonged to a family with the last name Picci. "See?" Siobhan said. "It's not just a ride. It's a piece of history."

"Whatever you say," Derick replied as they stepped onto the carousel and chose horses next to each other.

Siobhan was in awe. She'd never seen a carousel this beautiful. The ceiling had paintings of cherubs, and the horses all had intricate designs full of vibrant colors. Reds, lime greens, and lavenders were painted on Siobhan's horse. And next to her, sitting atop a blue and white one, was her knight in shining armor.

Even Derick smiled as the ride began. It was oddly satisfying to do something most people only do as children. The experience made her heart light in a way she hadn't felt in years.

As the ride began to speed up, the two looked ahead, watching the same scenery pass by again and again as they went around. Finally their eyes locked on each other, unable to focus on anything else. Because, despite the cool morning breeze, there was a warmth between them. Siobhan was happy. Being here with Derick in such a romantic city had intensified the love she'd already had for him, made her more conscious of how good they were together.

"Maybe you were right," Derick said.

"I'm always right," Siobhan replied with a smirk. "About what this time?"

"It's kind of fun," he said. "Going around and around with you."

She laughed softly, remembering how far they'd come since she'd moved back to New York. "You know, not too long ago you said you were done riding the merry-go-round with me."

The ride slowed down, and Derick reached his hand out so Siobhan could put her palm in his. He shrugged. "Guess I just realized I'd do anything as long as it's with you."

Chapter 35

THE TRIP HAD flown by. Before Siobhan knew it, their last day in Florence arrived. She stood in front of the open doors of their suite looking out over the gardens that separated them from the larger portion of the hotel. She was supposed to be getting ready—for what she had no idea—but she couldn't help staring at the trees and beautiful landscape that surrounded them.

Strong arms wrapped around her from behind, and she nestled back into them. "Let's move here," she said.

"Okay," Derick replied simply.

She laughed softly. "I'm kidding. If I find out you bought this place, I'm going to be seriously irritated."

He pressed a kiss into her hair. "No buying the Four Seasons. Got it."

They stood there together for a while, enjoying the simplicity of being together.

Finally, Derick spoke. "You need to get dressed." And with a soft pat on her ass, he moved away from her.

When she turned, she realized he was dressed in an expensive-looking blue suit she'd never seen before. "Where did you get that?"

"I bought it," he replied as he adjusted the cuff links on one wrist. "Do you like it?"

"Of course I like it. You look amazing." And he really did. The suit fit him in all the right ways, accentuating his broad shoulders and trim waist. "But if this place has a dress code that fancy, I'm going to be severely underdressed." Blaine had done a good job packing a bag for Siobhan, but unfortunately she hadn't thrown a ball gown into it.

"Did you look in the closet like I told you to?"

"Why would I? I know what's in there."

Derick rolled his eyes. "Obviously not." He walked over to the closet, opened the door and pulled out a garment bag. He made his way back over to her and handed it over.

"What's this?"

"Open it and find out." He grinned at her.

The smug bastard. Siobhan walked over to the bed and laid the bag on it so she could unzip it. Inside she found an elegant, strapless, burgundy dress in exactly her size. Her eyes snapped up to his.

"There should be matching shoes in there, too," he said as he examined himself in the mirror. "I'll leave you to it." Derick strode out of the room, leaving Siobhan to wonder if she wanted to kiss him or kill him.

She dressed quickly, savoring the way the soft satin draped around her. She took her time applying her makeup, wanting to look her best for the man she loved. Even if he did drive her crazy

90 percent of the time. She swept her hair to the side in a loose bun.

Once she was done, she went out to join him in the living room. He lifted his head when she approached and his eyes widened. "Wow."

Siobhan couldn't stop the smile that spread across her lips as she looked down at herself. "Guess that means you like it."

"Hell yeah I like it. Wow."

"You said that already."

"Leave me alone. I'm fantasizing."

"About?" she asked.

"Like I'm going to tell you," he scoffed.

"Well, that'd be pretty much par for the course since you haven't told me anything about tonight."

He slid his arms around her waist. "Hey, I let you pick what we did for the past five days. The least you can do is give me our last night to do what I want to do."

She rolled her eyes at him. "But I at least *told* you what we were doing."

He winked at her. "A guy's gotta have some secrets."

Siobhan laughed drily. "I'm pretty sure secrets are our worst enemies."

Tilting his head slightly, Derick seemed to contemplate that for a second. He said in a low voice, "I hope this one's different." Then he pulled away and grabbed a box from the coffee table. "Now for the pièce de résistance." He turned the box toward her before opening it.

Siobhan gasped as her hand flew to her chest. Inside was the most beautiful diamond necklace she'd ever seen. The diamonds were arranged to resemble flowers. The flowers were small at the clasp, but more and more were layered as they wound around to the front of the necklace. Once the diamonds reached where Siobhan imagined her collarbone would be, there were diamond pendants that hung down from the rows of flowers. Speechless, she looked up at Derick.

Allowing her a moment to inspect the necklace, he then removed it from the box, stepped behind her, and clasped it around her neck. He pressed a delicate kiss to her exposed nape.

Her fingers slid up and gently touched the jewels around her neck. "Derick, I—"

"I know you think it's a lot," he interrupted, his voice low and gravelly. "But for me, it's not even close to being enough. I wanted to get you something that would remind you of this trip, and I thought the flowers looked like the ones in the garden outside."

She turned toward him. "Derick, I'll never forget this trip. With or without a necklace. It's been perfect. *You've* been perfect. I can't possibly show you how much I appreciate all of this."

"Sure you can," he said through a smile. "You can accept the necklace."

She knew that, in some ways, by accepting the necklace she was accepting Derick. As himself. With no compromises. She took a deep breath and dropped her hand from where it had been touching the diamonds around her neck. "How do I look?"

He pressed his forehead to hers. "Exquisite."

Chapter 36

THE CAR TOOK them into the Piazza della Signoria, which Siobhan was fairly certain wasn't allowed since she hadn't seen a single other car in the square during any of their visits there. But Derick didn't seem concerned so she decided she wouldn't be, either.

They pulled up outside of the Palazzo Vecchio, a palace built in the thirteenth century. The driver opened the car door and Derick helped her out.

"What are we doing here?" Siobhan asked.

"You'll see," Derick said as he led her inside the palace. When they reached the stairs that would take them to the Arnolfo Tower, Derick stopped. "You want to take those off?" he asked, gesturing toward her shoes.

"No, I think I'll be okay."

He eyed her skeptically.

"What does that look mean? I've gotten much better at walking in heels recently."

He rubbed a hand over his short beard. "Okay. I'll walk behind you then. Go slow and please don't fall."

"Gee, thanks for that vote of confidence," she muttered as she slid past him and began her ascent up the stairs. Siobhan would never say it out loud, but by the time she'd reached the top, she'd wished she'd taken off her shoes.

Yet she didn't have long to focus on her aching feet, because in front of her stood a table for two surrounded by a circle of candles. The view from the tower was amazing, and the soft light that still emanated from the setting sun allowed her to see across the lit-up city of Florence to the mountains in the distance. Siobhan felt like a princess in that moment, high above a city she'd come to adore, gazing down at it with the man of her dreams. She whirled around toward Derick, to find him directly behind her.

Down on one knee.

Her body went still as her heart fluttered uncontrollably in her chest. *He isn't doing what I think he's doing. Is he?*

He held out a hand to her, and she instinctively took it. Derick gazed up at her, his expression serious but warm. "I've spent most of our time here trying to think of what I could say to convince you to spend the rest of your life with me, but I kept coming up empty. Because at the heart of it is the fact that I don't deserve you. No one does. You're beautiful, and brilliant, and dedicated, and talented. And I'm a guy who has a habit of doing and saying the wrong things."

Siobhan wanted to interrupt him—tell him he was crazy if he really thought that. But she knew that she'd ruined enough moments for him to last a lifetime. She wouldn't ruin any more.

He removed a small box from his pocket with the hand not

grasping hers. "So I figured my only chance was to bring you to the top of the highest place I could find, and make one more wish. I don't have a penny this time, though. I'm hoping that promising my heart is enough. I have one more diamond for you tonight. And my wish is that you'll agree to wear this one, too."

He flipped open the box, removed the ring, and held the beautiful square-cut diamond up to the hand he was holding.

"Siobhan Dempsey, I love you with everything that I am. Will you please let me be your husband?"

Derick looked up at her, waiting for her answer, and Siobhan wasn't even sure he was breathing. She felt her hand shaking in his grasp, but the ring remained steady.

She never would have imagined all those months ago that she'd fall into the arms of the one man she'd end up not being able to live without. It seemed perfect that all of the chaos and fighting that had prevented them from getting their relationship off the ground had led them to this: a serene and peaceful night on top of a tower.

And in that perfect moment came a simple word that floated in the breeze and wound itself around them both—intertwining them forever.

"Yes."

About the Authors

Elizabeth Hayley is actually "Elizabeth" and "Hayley," two friends who love reading romance novels to obsessive levels. This mutual love prompted them to put their English degrees to good use by penning their own romances.

HE'S WORTH MILLIONS, BUT HE'S WORTHLESS WITHOUT HER.

After a traumatic breakup with her billionaire boyfriend, Derick, Siobhan Dempsey moves to Detroit, where she can build her painting career on her own terms. But Derick wants her back. And though Siobhan's body comes alive at his touch, she doesn't know if she can trust him again....

THE GOLDEN BOY OF FOOTBALL JUST WENT *BAD*.

Quarterback Grayson Knight has a squeaky-clean reputation—
except when he's suddenly arrested for drug possession. Even
though she's on the opposing side of the courtroom, DA's
assistant Melissa St. James wants desperately to help him—and he
desperately wants her....

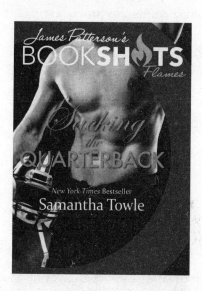

**Read about their thrilling affair in *Sacking the Quarterback*,
available now from**

THE BEAR MOUNTAIN DAYS ARE COLD, BUT THE NIGHTS ARE STEAMY....

Allie Fairchild made a mistake when she moved to Montana. Her rental is a mess, her coworkers at the trauma center are hostile, and her handsome landlord, Dex Belmont, is far from charming. But just when she's about to throw in the towel, life in Bear Mountain takes a surprisingly sexy turn....

Read the scorching romance, *Hot Winter Nights*, available now from

SPREAD YOUR WINGS AND SOAR.

Rigg Greensman is on the worst assignment of his life: filming a documentary about birds with "hot mess" scientist and host Sophie Castle. Rigg is used to the celebrity lifestyle, so he'd never be interested in down-to-earth Sophie. But he soon realizes she's got that sexy something that drives him wild…if only he can convince her to join him for the ride.

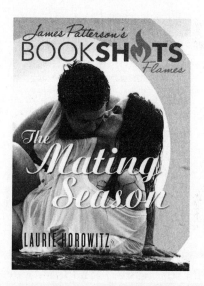

**Read the heart-pounding love story, *The Mating Season,*
available now from**

HER SECOND CHANCE AT LOVE MIGHT BE TOO GOOD TO BE TRUE....

When Chelsea O'Kane escapes to her family's inn in Maine, all she's got are fresh bruises, a gun in her lap, and a desire to start anew. That's when she runs into her old flame, Jeremy Holland. As he helps her fix up the inn, they rediscover what they once loved about each other.

Until it seems too good to last…

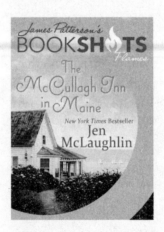

Read the stirring story of hope and redemption
The McCullagh Inn in Maine, **available now from**

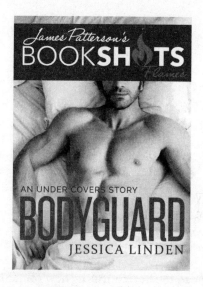

SHE NEVER EXPECTED TO FALL IN LOVE WITH A COWBOY....

Rodeo king Tanner Callen isn't looking to be tied down anytime soon. When he sees Madeline Harper at a local honky-tonk—even though everything about her screams New York City—he brings out every trick in his playbook to take her home.

But soon he learns that he doesn't just want her for a night.

Instead, he hopes for forever.

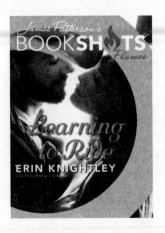

Read the heartwarming new romance
Learning to Ride, **available now from**

"I'M NOT ON TRIAL. SAN FRANCISCO IS."

Drug cartel boss the Kingfisher has a reputation for being violent and merciless. And after he's finally caught, he's set to stand trial for his vicious crimes—until he begins unleashing chaos and terror upon the lawyers, jurors, and police associated with the case. The city is paralyzed, and Detective Lindsay Boxer is caught in the eye of the storm.

Will the Women's Murder Club make it out alive—or will a sudden courtroom snare ensure their last breaths?

Read the shocking new Women's Murder Club story, available now only from

BOOK**SHOTS**

SOME GAMES AREN'T FOR CHILDREN....

After a nasty divorce, Christy Moore finds her escape in Marty Hawking, who introduces her to all sorts of experiences, including an explosive new game called "Make-Believe."

But what begins as innocent fun soon turns dark, and as Marty pushes the boundaries further and further, the game just may end up deadly.

**Read the new jaw-dropping thriller, *Let's Play Make-Believe,*
available now from**

BOOK**SHOTS**